WHAT STAYS BURIED

WHAT STAYS BURIED

BURIED

SUZANNE YOUNG

HARPER

An Imprint of HarperCollinsPublishers

Library of Congress Control Number: 2022940764
ISBN 978-0-06-325712-2

Typography by Chris Kwon
23 24 25 26 27 LBC 5 4 3 2 1
❖
First Edition

In loving memory of my grandmother Josephine Parzych.
Grateful for every moment.

CALISTA WYNN KNEW the boy was dead before she even opened her eyes. He whispered her name again, soft and far away, how all ghosts sound even when they're right next to your ear. An echo through the veil of this life and the otherworld.

Calista's eyes fluttered open, but she didn't turn to the boy right away. It was too early for a communication. Most ghosts had the decency to let her sleep until her alarm sounded for school. She hadn't been sleeping well, not these past few weeks, at least. She would have appreciated another fifteen minutes of rest.

Finally, already awake, Calista turned on her side without lifting her head off the pillow. Right there, inches away, was a pale-faced kid with cropped blond hair and dark blue eyes. The collar of his shirt was stiff with speckles of blood.

"You can see me, right?" the boy asked, hopeful. Calista felt a stab of sympathy for him. He'd probably been searching for a medium for years, decades, before finding her. That was usually how it worked. Word of mouth in the ghost world took awhile. It wasn't like they could text.

"Yeah, I can see you," Calista said, sitting up.

She cracked her neck and blinked her eyes open wider, sleep still on the corners of her vision. Morning sunlight filtered through her bedroom curtains as a prism of colors danced on her ceiling from a hanging suncatcher. Cast in blues and purples, Calista shivered once in the chilly air before turning back to the boy. Ghosts always brought the cold with them.

"How can I help you?" Calista asked, her voice coming out with white puffs of air.

The spirit smiled, a little kid's smile, although he'd probably been Calista's age when he died, thirteen or fourteen, she guessed. "I . . ." the boy started, and then furrowed his blond brows. "I don't know," he said. "I've been looking for someone. . . . I forgot why."

This was also not unusual. After a while, ghosts began to forget things, much like the living. Although ghosts were stuck at the age they had been when they died, they kept . . . going. *Imagine spending seventy years as a fourteen-year-old boy?* Calista thought. *Yikes.*

"Are you looking for your mom?" Calista asked. This was typically the case with boys, searching for their mother's care. A kiss on a bruised knee.

The ghost's face lit up. "Yes," he said, smiling. "Yes, my

mom! Can you help me find my mom?"

Calista exhaled heavily. She had no idea what time period this boy was from—it was hard to tell sometimes. With the exception of the '80s, hairstyles didn't change too drastically, especially for boys. And it was entirely possible that this ghost's mother had already passed away years before, and that would make things difficult. Not all of the departed became ghosts.

Calista noticed the time on her alarm clock and reached to switch it off before it could sound. "Why don't you come back after school?" she suggested to the spirit. "I'll help you then." She could at least point him to some other relatives if his mother was no longer around.

The boy stared blankly at Calista, maybe forgetting the concept of mornings and going to school. She pointed toward the window. "You go," she said clearly. "And I'll summon you when I get home."

He nodded, disappointed, but seeming to understand. And then, the boy evaporated.

Calista sat there a moment, the room warming now that the spirit was gone. She was tempted to lie back down, sleep that extra fifteen minutes, but it would take her at least that long to fall asleep again. It was time to start the day.

She got out of bed and headed toward the shower, yawning as she scratched at her messy black hair. *In a week, I won't have to deal with dead boys anymore*, she thought. But the second it crossed her mind, grief lay heavy on her chest. She could dress up the idea all she liked, but Calista didn't want to lose her gift. It was part of who she was. She'd be losing herself.

Calista Wynn had discovered she was a medium the same way most mediums did: as a child—in Calista's particular case, in the bathtub, just as a ghost began massaging shampoo into her hair from behind. That extra set of fingers touching hers through the suds, that moment of confusion . . . Are these *my* fingers? Are these . . . ?

Followed by screaming. Shouting. And a dead woman smiling at her from the floor of her bathroom in a Victorian-era burial dress.

Oh, yeah. That was the fun part. Sometimes, ghosts could touch her.

After that, Calista began seeing ghosts all the time. She'd known it was coming, of course. She was descended from a long line of mediums on her father's side. It was weird enough, being from a family that talks to ghosts. But even weirder was that, although they were powerful, the only spiritual mediums left in the Wynn family were the children.

Calista's grandmother claimed it started after she lost her daughter many years ago. But Calista's mother, Nora, who didn't possess any supernatural gifts, suggested it was more likely something in their genes. Either way, there was one hard truth that had become apparent: at thirteen years old, all of the mediums in the Wynn family lost their ability to see ghosts. It had happened to Calista's father, Mac, and to all five of his younger siblings. And soon, it would happen to her. Sure, the Wynns still had other gifts, other intuitions, but the ghosts stopped appearing to them.

Calista had one more week of seeing ghosts until her birthday. And then . . . Well, she didn't want to think about then.

"Molly," Calista called, fighting back another yawn. "It's time for school." She knocked on her little sister's bedroom door at the same time she opened it. Molly was six years old, the kind of six where she talked like a mini-mom, reading picture books to a party of stuffed bears, reminding Calista to do the dishes, and—

Calista stood frozen in the doorway of her little sister's bedroom. The sheets were folded back neatly, but Molly was nowhere in sight. Logically, Calista knew that Molly had probably gotten up and poured herself some cereal, munching on Lucky Charms and watching the local news until cartoons came on. But that wasn't her way. Molly could "sleep like the dead," her mother always quipped. Molly had to be dragged from her bed every morning, no exceptions. Mediums slept hard, and Molly was just about ready to come into her gifts.

Unlike the abrupt ending of the gift, the beginning of a medium's powers started slowly. Certain feelings emerged, and ways of knowing things they shouldn't. And then, one day, a ghost would just . . . appear to them. Unsettling, sure. But also exhilarating.

Molly hadn't seen any ghosts yet—Calista was certain

of that. But her little sister was having headaches, tingling hands and feet. A taste of metal in her mouth that she told Calista was like licking a 9-volt battery. Calista didn't ask her how she knew what licking a 9-volt battery tasted like or, for that matter, how she knew what a 9-volt battery was. Mediums, sometimes they just knew things.

And although it would be fun for Molly to develop her gifts, it only reminded Calista that she was losing hers. It wasn't enough time. It would never be enough.

"Molly," Calista called again, checking the room one more time before turning to face the hallway. Their mother, Nora, left early for work, which made it Calista's job to wake up Molly each morning and walk her to the bus. Calista didn't mind. Things had been tough around the house for the last few years. It was the least she could do. "Molly?" Calista yelled, heading toward the kitchen.

She heard the faint sound of a video playing, and the tension in her body eased slightly. Molly must have snuck in to get Calista's phone from the nightstand while she was asleep. She was probably at the counter, watching videos. Although . . . the rest of the house was unusually quiet.

Calista staggered to a stop, looking around the hall. "Dad?" she said. When there was no response, she moved to the staircase leading up to the bedrooms. "Dad?" she repeated, gripping the banister to lean over and peer through the slotted rails. "Gran?"

It was quiet. Calista's heart began to beat faster.

Where is everyone?

She pushed her hair away from her face and rushed toward the kitchen. Sure enough, Calista's phone was on the counter, playing an online video about ghost hunting, of all things, but her sister was nowhere to be found.

Calista searched the living room, and just before she got to the stairs again to go up to the attic, she noticed the front door slightly ajar. Her stomach dipped with fresh fear. She ran onto the porch, barefoot and wearing a mismatched pajama ensemble. The wood slats were freezing under her toes, and she quickly looked around the yard.

The grass was coated in a white dusting of frost, the air biting with cold. Calista shivered, wrapping her arms around herself. But then she looked down the block and saw Molly at the corner, still in pink llama pajamas, cradling one of her stuffed bears.

"Molly!" Calista screamed. Just then, her father, Mac, rushed over from the side of the house. Her dad's eyes were wide with fear.

"Did you find her?" Mac asked, but Calista ran past him down the block. "She found her!" Calista heard her father say to Grandma Josie, who was shuffling out from the basement door.

"Thank goodness," Grandma Josie muttered, sounding relieved.

But Calista was not relieved. How long had her sister been outside? It was freezing. The closer she got, the more she realized that Molly wasn't scared. She was smiling, talking to someone.

There was no one else there.

Calista slowed her steps, searching for an otherworldly figure—a ghost of some sort. Seeing nothing, she worried momentarily that she'd already lost her gift. Molly waved toward the street, and then turned to Calista.

"Hi, Callie," Molly said with a smile, her missing front tooth visible.

When Calista reached her, she bent down on one knee. Above the girls, a jet from the nearby airport rumbled the air like thunder. Calista began rubbing her sister's arms to warm her. She checked around again, but still saw no one— alive or dead.

"Molly, who were you talking to?" she asked when the plane was gone.

"You didn't see her?" Molly asked, indignant that Calista might have missed something important.

"No," Calista said, taking Molly's cold hand to start back toward the house. Calista noticed her father and grand- mother waiting on the front lawn, their expressions strained with worry. "I didn't see anyone, Molly," she said, looking down at her. "Who was it?"

"I don't know," Molly said. "But I call her the Tall Lady." She glanced up at Calista and smiled, her brown eyes wide and excited. "She was beautiful," Molly added with a lisp, fluttering out the bottom of her pajama top as if it were a dress. "And she told me she's been looking for a little girl *just like me.*"

Molly beamed, but Calista was more than a little bothered. Definitely confused. She didn't doubt that her little sister was telling the truth—Molly would never lie. But it still didn't make any sense.

Fact was, Calista couldn't see this Tall Lady. As they arrived back at the house, she knew that her gifts were still working just fine, so why couldn't she see this spirit too? It could mean only one thing: the Tall Lady was hiding from her.

Why would a ghost do that?

2

CALISTA WASN'T SURE where to start with explaining to her father that her little sister had almost been kidnapped by a ghost lady, so she went ahead and just said it.

"Molly was lured outside by a ghost," Calista said to her father. "Molly calls her the Tall Lady, and apparently, the ghost told Molly that she'd been 'looking for a little girl just like her,'" Calista added, making air quotes with her fingers.

Mac stared at her for a long moment before beginning to pace the living room.

"She was a ghost?" he asked, looking back at Calista. "But *you* didn't see her?"

"No," Calista said, shaking her head. "And honestly . . . I'm not sure how Molly saw her either. I was nearly seven when I saw my first ghost." She lowered her voice. "Do you think her gift has developed early?" Calista glanced toward the hall leading to Molly's bedroom, where her sister was getting herself dressed for school. "She hasn't seen any *other* ghosts," she told her father pointedly.

Her father seemed to think it over, and then looked to where his mother was sitting in her red velvet easy chair, tapping her feet on the floor as she rocked her body. "What about you, Mom?" he asked. "Any thoughts?"

"My thoughts," Grandma Josie said, "are that your daughters are going to be late for school. This nonsense will be here when they get back."

Calista's grandmother, one of the best mediums to ever inhabit the state of New York, thought schooling was the most important aspect of living. She'd been telling Calista since she was Molly's age that nothing should come before a strong education. Boring, but not terrible advice. Although their family had lived in Meadowmere for generations, the small town was falling apart, quite literally sinking into the marshes along the Hook River. Grandma Josie was hoping the girls would eventually see their way out. The best way to do that was with an education.

Mac laughed and turned back to his daughter. "Well, there you have it," he said with a shrug. "You head off to school and I'll look into this 'Tall Lady.' We'll discuss it again when you get home."

Calista reluctantly agreed and began to walk away, but then she snapped her fingers and turned around. "Oh, Gran," she said. "Would you mind helping me with a charm? There was another boy in my room this morning when I woke up."

"I swear . . . ," Grandma Josie said, shaking her head. "You'd think there was a flashing neon sign that reads 'Dead Boys This Way' and an arrow pointing straight to you."

Mac snorted a laugh and Calista smiled at her father before leaving to get ready for school.

On her way to her room, Calista checked in on Molly. She found her sister trying to tie her own shoes. She had almost figured it out.

"Five minutes," Calista told her as a reminder that they were running late.

"Don't rush me!" Molly said in a determined voice, undoing the loose knot in her shoelace to start over.

Calista smiled and went to get ready for school.

Molly had provided only a few more details about her interaction with the Tall Lady. The ghost first appeared in the kitchen window when Molly was about to pour some cereal and beckoned her outside. The spirit had black hair, ruby-red lips, and a beautiful yellow dress. And of course, Molly said she was really tall, easily as tall as their father. Molly and the spirit had gone for a walk, and that was when Calista had discovered her sister on the corner.

Calista got into her bedroom and pulled on a flowered top and jeans, slipping her feet into fleece-lined boots. Her backpack was thrown in the corner, and Calista realized with a bit of panic that she had forgotten to do her English homework. She'd meant to do it this morning, but between the boy in her room and her missing sister, she'd lost track of time. Maybe she could finish it in homeroom.

As Calista picked up the wide-toothed comb from her dresser and began to drag it through her thick hair, she considered the events again. The entire experience with Molly was majorly creepy. She'd already made her sister promise not to follow any more ghosts outside, but Calista was still bothered.

Why couldn't Calista see the Tall Lady? What did it mean?

"Callie, come on!" Molly called from the hallway, sounding very put out. "It's been more than five minutes!"

Calista laughed and set down her comb before looping her backpack over one shoulder. She walked into the hallway, following an anxious Molly as she led them toward the door, her shoelaces still loose but otherwise correctly tied. Calista helped Molly zip her jacket before grabbing her own from the hook by the door.

"See you later, Dad, Gran," Calista said toward the living room. Grandma Josie nodded from her chair and Mac held up his hand in a wave.

"Bye-bye!" Molly called vaguely into the air.

When the sisters got onto the front porch, Calista noticed the big yellow bus pull to the stop at the end of the street. They ran for it, Molly's puppy-dog backpack bouncing and rattling with loose items.

They made it there on time, but Molly gave Calista a disappointed-mom look anyway as she bolted up the bus steps. Calista waved to her sister through the window while the bus hissed and then pulled away.

Once Molly was safely off to school, Calista began her cold walk to Kennedy Middle School. She pulled her jacket tightly around herself, noting the crispness in the morning air. Luckily school was only a few blocks away. Most days, Calista didn't mind the walk. It gave her a chance to think, a chance for some quiet, since ghosts didn't typically accost her in public. But as she passed through the quiet downtown of Meadowmere, the storefronts still dark and rolled newspapers waiting on the stoops, the hairs on the back of Calista's neck stood on end.

There was a crackling noise, like the sound of electricity on a power line. A vibration growing closer, looming just behind her. It felt dangerous.

Calista spun around, but the street was deserted. A gust of wind rustled the branches of a nearby tree, and there was the unsettling caw from a crow atop one of the buildings. Calista swallowed hard, feeling wary and nervous. Almost . . . Almost like she was being followed.

She practically ran the last block to school, blending into the small crowd of students waiting for the bell. When Calista looked back the way she'd come, she searched for a figure in a beautiful yellow dress. She was relieved when no one was there. Despite this, Calista felt a negative charge in the air, a strong pulse. She spun back around and quickly dashed toward the school.

Calista Wynn had nothing in common with the flesh and blood kids at her school, a fact that was profoundly obvious as she darted her gaze around the small cafeteria in fifth period. As the other kids laughed and tossed soggy french fries at one another, she was left out almost entirely. She wouldn't mind being in on the joke once in a while.

Not that the other kids were mean to her—this was a "nice town," her grandmother would no doubt tell her after school. But Calista was an outsider, even though her family had lived here for generations. The Wynns were the family that others only came to visit when they were in trouble or in search of something that couldn't normally be found.

Most of the time, Calista didn't mind being alone. Although she was hardly really alone with all the ghosts stopping to chat. But there were other days, like today, when she could feel it in her bones—a loneliness that was cold and achy. A weight of grief that lay heavy in her chest.

She was on the brink of what felt like a terrible tragedy that no one outside of her family could ever understand.

Calista sat at an empty table near the foggy glass of the window. It overlooked the rotting remains of a playground, half-sunken into the soil, with marsh weeds covering the bottom of the slide. Kennedy used to be a K–12 school, but after last year's redistricting, it was now a sixth through eighth grade middle school. It would be her last year in the run-down lunchroom before heading to the newly built high school.

It seemed so odd to have a new building in such an old

town. Sticking out like a sore thumb. Grandma Josie said it was just the start of the city coming to take over, but she'd been saying that for years, and all they'd gotten was a high school and a Duane Reade. Calista wouldn't have minded a little more growth.

But then that idea scratched her nerves in an insistent way. *Change.* Her thirteenth birthday was just around the corner and she'd never feared anything so much in her whole life. Meanwhile, the other girls in her class were throwing parties, excited for their milestone. But for Calista, turning thirteen meant something entirely different. It was an ending. One that smelled of wet mud and soot.

A chicken nugget sailed past Calista's head, and her attention snapped to a table across the room. Wyland Davis immediately winced and held up his hand in apology. Calista turned to find a table of girls giggling to each other. They then looked over at Wyland, pretending to be upset that he would throw food at them. Moira Grace looked right through Calista as if she didn't exist.

Calista drooped slightly, casting one last glance in Wyland's direction in time to see his eyebrows pull together, as if thinking something of her. But then his friend bumped his shoulder, handing him another bit of nugget fuel, and Calista was forgotten.

She looked down at her tray of food, wishing she had someone to text aside from her mother. At least when she went home later, her dad and grandmother would be there.

And she supposed she could summon the ghost boy from this morning. At least he wanted to talk to her.

"Did you hear?" Peter Oslo said to his friend Augie as they paused with their lunch trays just beyond Calista's table. "Another kid went missing."

Calista's ears perked up as she watched them, listening intently. Peter and Augie were soccer players for the local team. While Peter was very short with spiky brown hair, Augie had the distinction of having been the tallest kid in their grade for three years running.

"That's the second kid gone," Augie said in a hushed voice. "They haven't even found that Winters kid yet. I bet he's dead."

Calista leaned closer to listen. She had only vaguely heard about Devon Winters running away last week. He lived on the other side of town and attended the Catholic school there. His story hadn't even been on the news. Then again, few things in Meadowmere were deemed important enough for the television stations anymore. But now a second missing person? Calista felt her heart begin to race.

"Don't say he's dead," Peter whispered to Augie, clearly alarmed at the thought. But then both boys ducked their heads and lowered their voices, as if conspirators. "Listen," Peter continued. "It's not public yet, but you know my dad's a cop. I heard him talking on the phone. At first, they thought Winters ran away, but now with this new kid missing . . ." He shook his head. "He called it a pattern. My dad said they don't have any suspects either."

"Who was it?" Calista asked out loud, startling both Peter and Augie.

Her mind was racing through the possibilities, different feelings pinging in her chest. She couldn't help but think of the boy in her room this morning. Although with his memory loss, she thought he'd been dead for too long to be the new missing kid. Still, she wondered if it could be connected.

"Who's the second person missing?" Calista clarified for Peter.

Peter curled his lip at her interruption, upset that she'd been listening. "None of your business, Calista," he said, not unkindly, but in a tone to let her know he wouldn't give her any more information.

But now the hairs on Calista's arms were standing on end, a bit of sickness swirling in her stomach. She'd find out the details of the missing kid soon enough. She could feel it coming, smell it, even—the sweet smell of lilac perfume, of musky cologne.

New visitors would be arriving at her house. Calista had little doubt that it would be the parents of those missing kids, hoping for her help.

Although the town generally liked to ignore the Wynns, when they began to lose hope, they always came knocking on her door. Only Calista wasn't sure she'd have the answers they were looking for.

3

THE SMALL WHITE house at 11 Marble Lane was set back from the road with a long driveway flanked on either side by soaring elm trees. The branches swayed in the wind as Calista made her way toward her front porch. Coming home was like waking up for her—a time when she could truly be herself. She cracked a smile. Molly wouldn't be home for another hour, so this was her quiet time with her family.

Calista bounded up the steps as a jet flew low overhead, rumbling loudly. Just as she got to the door, Calista stopped short when she noticed a business card tucked into the edge of the screen.

The smell of musky cologne, the same scent she'd smelled earlier in the cafeteria, drifted into her nose. She plucked out the card, tingling racing over her skin as she read the name: Jerimiah Winters, Realtor. But under his name was a note scratched in red ink.

Need to talk to you. Please.

Calista felt a wave of dizziness, and she gripped the door handle to steady herself. There was pain associated with the card, desperation. She recognized the name, of course— Winters. The father of the first missing boy.

Thirteen-year-old Devon Winters had gone missing a week ago. Like Peter had said at school, the police originally thought he'd run away. But with the amount of grief radiating from this card, Calista knew that his father didn't believe that rumor to be true. And according to Peter, the police didn't believe it anymore either.

Calista tucked the card into her back pocket and walked inside the house.

The moment she stepped into the foyer, Grandma Josie appeared, standing there with a braided shawl over her shoulders. Her thin gray hair was fluffed around her head in a white halo. She was teeming with energy, worked up about something.

"Hi there, sweetie," her grandmother said, her voice scratchy. She shuffled over to stop just a few feet away, a smile plastered across her wrinkled skin, pulling it into happy lines around her mouth. "How was your day?"

Just as Calista opened her mouth to answer, her grandmother motioned toward the kitchen and cut her off.

"Because your father is gettin' on my last nerve," Grandma

Josie said loud enough for him to overhear. "I *told* him there is no tomato sauce in that soup."

Calista's father laughed good-naturedly from the kitchen. "And I told the old woman," Mac sang out, "that there most certainly is. So here we are."

Normally Calista didn't mind their little arguments over food, stories her mother would beg her to relay word for word when she got home, but today wasn't a good day. First, she'd been worried that Molly had nearly been kidnapped, and then she found out two boys had *actually* been kidnapped. Now a father was searching for answers too. More would come. She needed to gather information.

Calista dropped her backpack next to the door and moved past her grandmother into the hall.

"Where are you going?" Grandma Josie asked, sounding hurt. "You haven't even told me about your day yet."

"Sorry, Gran, but I need to talk to Dad for a minute." Calista looked around quickly for her father. "Dad, did you find out anything about the Tall Lady?" she asked, waiting for him.

Mac came out from the kitchen wearing the same plaid flannel shirt and heavy boots that he had worn on his last day of work. His handsome face was grayish as concern tugged down the edges of his mouth.

"Nothing yet," he said, and paused. "You don't look well," he added. "Did something else happen? Is Molly okay?"

"Molly's fine," Calista said. "She's still at school, I—" She paused, rubbing her temple. She would eventually tell them about the missing kids, of course—she'd need their help. But a sudden headache banged against her temples, and her stomach felt sick and uneasy. This had been happening more often. The last gasps of her gift fighting to stay.

"Oh, honey," her dad said, stooping down to examine her.

Just then, the front door swung open wildly, bumping into the wall behind it. They all turned as Calista's mother, Nora, stood half-bent over with grocery bags in both arms. She smiled at Calista, tendrils of dark hair hanging around her face.

"A little help?" Nora asked with a laugh.

Calista blinked away the headache into a dull throb, and then quickly took one of the paper bags from her mother's arms. Her father leaned over her shoulder to see if he could peek inside the bag.

"Ask her if she got the tomato sauce for the soup," he said anxiously. Grandma Josie cursed behind him, mumbling that he was wrong.

"Did you get the tomato sauce?" Calista asked her mother. Nora laughed and glanced around the room.

"That your father?" she asked. "Tell him there is no sauce in that chicken soup recipe."

"Told you," Grandma Josie said, proudly adjusting her shawl around her shoulders.

Calista's father beamed and crossed to his wife, standing

close to her. "Tell her she looks beautiful today," he said warmly.

"No," Calista replied, scrunching up her nose. Nora smiled anyway, guessing what her husband had said.

"I'll be in the kitchen," her mother announced.

And as she headed that way, Nora walked right through Calista's father. His spirit reassembled quickly, and he was still watching after his wife lovingly. Calista stared at him for a long moment, memorizing his features. In just under a week, she wouldn't be able to see her dad anymore either. All the ghosts would be gone.

Calista's father and her grandma Josie would soon disappear from her life. And at the thought of losing them, the ache in her bones deepened. It was unbearable to think about. So . . . she didn't. Calista hadn't let herself think about losing them at all.

"You can't let your grief control you," her aunt Freya had told her once. Calista had taken that advice to heart, using it to stay focused and strong. It was what her family needed most from her.

Although Calista had been seeing her grandma Josie's spirit since she was eight or so, Mac Wynn had died suddenly and tragically in a work accident just two years prior—a devastating loss to the entire neighborhood, but especially to his family.

At his funeral, Calista's aunt Freya had stayed by her

side. She was a stunning woman, tall and stylish enough to be in a magazine. She wore a chic black hat with thin netting draped over her face and gold bracelets jangling on her wrists. Calista was sure she'd never known anyone as beautiful as her aunt Freya, no one as naturally powerful. Her gift flowed around her like a warm current, vibrating with energy, even if she couldn't see ghosts anymore.

After the service, Calista stood a respectful distance from her father's casket as her mother sobbed in a front row chair, Molly with a neighbor in the back of the room. Suddenly, Aunt Freya grabbed Calista's hand and squeezed it tightly. She turned to look up at her aunt.

"I know you don't feel like crying now because your father isn't gone to you," Aunt Freya said, her voice thick as honey. "But one day he will be, Calista. It's a blessing for you, this delayed grief. Because right now, your family needs you. They need someone who can see both sides of the veil, and that's you. Your job is to protect your family and smother your mama and Molly with love. You understand that?"

"Yes," Calista said. And she did. Her mother's grief would have buried her otherwise. She couldn't endure the sorrow of loss at the same time as her mother, not when she knew she had to protect her and Molly.

"Good," Aunt Freya told her. "And one day, you'll need your mother and your sister in return. But that time isn't now. It's time to be strong. You can't let your grief control you. Promise me?"

"I promise," Calista said, agreeing.

Freya's expression weakened at the answer as she pressed her mouth into a sympathetic smile. Then she nodded her approval, squeezing Calista's hand one more time before letting it drop.

"Good," Freya said definitively. "Very good." She turned to stare at the casket, tears glistening in her eyes. "And you be sure to tell my brother Mac that I'll miss him something fierce," she added in a shaky voice before walking away.

Calista stood there a moment, never letting her gaze touch on her father's casket. Refusing to acknowledge it there. There was no sense in that. Mac's spirit was at home, waiting for her to come back. She didn't need closure. She still had him. Instead, she would do exactly as she promised her aunt Freya. She would be strong.

And in the time since, she'd done just that. With her father's help, Calista had been able to help her mother navigate switching over bills, file receipts, find the missing things she needed. Calista was Mac's voice, and then, as time went on, the family fell into a routine. Calista had her father all to herself—never losing even a moment with him. And she stayed strong, just as she had promised. She watched over her mother and her sister.

Suddenly, the television set clicked on by itself in the living room. Calista and her father both looked over from the foyer while Grandma Josie adjusted her shawl, moving forward curiously. A news program was playing, and

Calista took a step into the room.

"A second boy has been reported missing in the small area of Meadowmere," the news announcer said, sympathy painting his expression. "Thirteen-year-old Thomas Hassel was reported missing by his mother early yesterday morning after he disappeared from his bedroom sometime in the night."

An image came on the television screen and Calista gasped, falling back a step. She'd been right to wonder about the missing boy earlier. She recognized him—but not from her school.

"What's wrong?" Mac asked, looking down at his daughter.

"I know him," she replied. "I . . ." Calista swung around to face her father. Her grandmother shuffled into the room, alarmed at her tone.

"Who do you know?" Grandma Josie asked, darting a look at the TV and squinting her eyes.

"That missing boy," Calista said. "He's the one who was in my room this morning. Only he didn't seem recently deceased," she pointed out. "He couldn't even remember why he was there. Which means . . . Wait, what does that mean?" she asked, turning to her grandmother.

Grandma Josie swallowed hard, the corners of her mouth pulling downward. Calista's heart beat faster at the concern on her face.

"It means you should go get my books," Grandma Josie murmured. "Meadowmere has a big problem."

NOT ALL GHOSTS understood they were dead. Calista had known that, going back to the first few she'd spoken to. Most of the time, those who came to her were boys— she didn't know why. Her grandmother had explained to her once that more boys died in accidents: drowning, snow-mobiling, skateboarding—a lot of head injuries. Because of the trauma and the shock, many of them didn't pass on to the other side right away. They hung about, looking for their families. Looking for their mothers.

The boy Calista had spoken to this morning seemed more lost than most. She should have guessed immediately that his death had been . . . traumatic. She'd only seen it once or twice before, but murder—it damaged the memory of ghosts, erased that moment from them. It was why they could rarely remember their killers, which was frustrating for their families.

Now Calista wished she'd spoken to Thomas more when he'd appeared to her this morning. She felt downright guilty for dismissing him.

Calista fetched Grandma Josie's stack of books from the basement—volumes of the Wynn family history—and raced them upstairs. While her mother hummed from the kitchen, oblivious as she started dinner, Calista returned to the living room.

Grandma Josie was in her chair, rocking and tapping her small feet on the floor. Calista knelt down and spread out the volumes of books along the rug, waiting for her grandmother to direct her.

As Grandma Josie scanned the book covers, Calista turned to her father.

"I think the boy was murdered," Calista said quietly. Mac's expression sagged with grief. "Thomas was very confused," Calista continued. "And he still had blood on his shirt. I thought he was an old spirit at first, but now I realize he just didn't know he was dead yet. And that might mean . . . that could mean he was murdered, right?"

Calista didn't speak to many murder victims; they typically sought out the help of older mediums. Although Calista was just as good, if not better, a lot of adults—even the dead ones—had trouble connecting with child mediums on the topic. And the fact was, most murder victims were adults.

"That sort of memory loss could indicate murder, yes," Mac agreed.

He looked at his mother. She nodded at him, and then pointed one of her shaky fingers at volume six. This surprised

Calista because that was a volume they'd never used before. She wondered what was in it.

"About halfway through," Grandma Josie said, watching attentively as Calista pulled the book in front of her. "There's a section on lost souls in there." She paused, her dark eyes growing damp. "Be ready for what's to come," she added in a whisper. "Because there's nothing more tragic than the loss of a child."

The room grew quiet, and Calista knew that Grandma Josie was speaking from experience. Even though her grandmother was no longer in this realm, Calista felt her heavy grief just the same. The weight of the family tragedy.

Virginia Wynn had been Calista's aunt, although she'd never met her. Her father's older sister was an incredible child medium, powerful and well-known throughout town—even so far as New York City. Grandma Josie said she was the strongest medium in the family and on pace to grow even more powerful as an adult. But tragically, on her thirteenth birthday . . . Virginia disappeared.

Grandma Josie didn't like to talk about it much, and Mac had been too little to remember the details. But from what Calista had heard in hushed whispers from relatives over the years, the police found Virginia's body exactly thirteen days after she'd gone missing. She died of natural causes, they said. But Grandma Josie never quite believed that.

For years, right up until she passed away, Grandma Josie attempted to contact her daughter on the other side of the veil. But Virginia never showed up, not even when summoned. Mac tried to convince Grandma Josie to stop looking, saying that Virginia must have already moved on. It was a sore spot in the family history, their own brand of unspeakable tragedy. And partly, it was why other local families still came to them when their own loved ones went missing. They knew that the Wynns understood the stakes. But it had been a long time since someone went missing in Meadowmere. A long time until now.

"Right there," Grandma Josie said, stopping her rocking to sit forward in the chair.

Calista looked down at the open page and saw the section labeled "Lost Souls." There was a folded piece of loose paper with yellowed edges. Calista opened it and saw an old, hand-drawn map of the marshes, an X marking a spot. Calista tucked the paper into the next page and read the section of the book Grandma Josie had pointed out. There was an explanation on lost souls written in black ink, listing things to expect. But Calista knew immediately that wasn't the part she was supposed to read. Almost glowing on the side of the page was frantic writing in blue ink, outlined in red—pulsing with pain. Calista had to turn the book sideways to read it.

The Curse of Virginia Wynn

Calista felt her stomach drop, a prickle of fear. Mac asked her to read the section out loud. It seemed as though he'd never encountered it before either. Grandma Josie sat silently, watching on. Calista took a breath and began reading to the room.

"The death of Virginia Wynn began a curse on the entire Wynn family. The thirteen by thirteen curse strips mediums of their ability to mature into their full gifts. It is done by taking the most powerful in the family at age thirteen and sacrificing them within this symbol." Calista paused to look over the drawing next to the words. It was a circle with three wavy red lines and ten sharply pointed shapes inside it. Even though it was just a drawing, the symbol felt . . . evil. Calista swallowed hard and continued reading.

"Before they reach their full potential," she said, "and after being held between the veils of the living and the dead, the sacrifices are killed on the thirteenth day. The curse is quite unbreakable. The soul of the sacrificed is damned to— to *limbo* for eternity, holding the curse in place."

Calista gasped, looking up at her grandmother. Mac put his palm over his mouth, horrified at the words. As a medium, being sent to limbo was a fate worse than death. No way to cross over. No way to communicate. Nothingness forever. A true lost soul.

"Why didn't you tell me?" Mac asked quietly, turning to his mother. Grandma Josie's lips were pursed together tightly as she held back her emotion.

"Because I don't believe anything is permanent," Grandma Josie said, casting a sharp look in his direction.

"And if I told you she was in limbo, I worried you'd stop looking for your sister. We can't give up, Mac. We can't ever give up on Virginia."

"Oh, Mom," Mac said sadly, "I never did. I always kept looking, even when I didn't say." He reached for his mother to grip her hand, able to connect on the spirit plane. She nodded at him, offering a sad smile.

"After Virginia was killed," Grandma Josie said, turning back to Calista, "that's when the Wynn family lost their ability to communicate with the dead after the age of thirteen. All six of my other children, including your father. And their children throughout the country. Those who were already adults at the time of the curse lived out their days just fine—I was able to keep most of my gifts right up until the moment I stopped breathing. But I never could find my daughter's spirit. And now, this curse is about to steal your gifts, as well."

Calista hadn't really understood she was under a curse up until that moment. It made her even more indignant at the thought of her abilities being stripped away. It felt even more unfair.

"Whatever is happening to those missing boys," Grandma Josie continued, "is not a coincidence. Two thirteen-year-olds going missing in Meadowmere is a sign. A warning. A threat of things to come."

"From who?" Calista asked. "We have to figure out who or what is behind this. If kids are dying . . ." She swallowed hard and her grandmother frowned and looked away.

The worry in her grandmother's expression frightened Calista. How many more kids would disappear in her town? Were all the children of Meadowmere in danger?

Although Calista felt invisible in her town on most days, it was still her home. And she would defend it. She would defend her family, curse or not.

"We'll find out what happened to those boys and see where it leads us," Calista added, drawing her grandmother's attention again. "And then . . . maybe then you'll know what happened to Aunt Virginia."

· Grandma Josie opened her mouth to speak, then immediately shut it without saying a word. Calista got the sense that the old woman had more to share, but considering the heavy mood in the room, she didn't think it was the right time to press for more information. Her intuition told her that her questions would go unanswered.

Calista closed the volume, decided.

"We'll summon Thomas Hassel tonight," she told them. "Piece together what happened to him."

Just then, a yellow school bus passed by the front window on its way to the stop. Molly would walk in the door any moment. Calista didn't want her little sister to know about the missing kids just yet. And she definitely didn't want her to know about the curse. She needed answers first. Calista always did her best to keep her sister's life as normal as possible, considering that eventually, it would become exceedingly abnormal.

"We'll make the plan after dinner," Calista added, gathering up the books. She'd leave them in her room for now.

As Calista stood, her father seemed lost in thought while Grandma Josie turned back to the news program. It had moved on to the weather—rain was expected. But Calista didn't think Grandma Josie was really watching it anyway. Sadness continued to radiate off of her.

She missed Virginia.

For now, Calista would put aside the idea of curses and summoning. She wanted time to think on it, what it could mean. She even had a small hope that it could give her a way to keep her gifts. But it was a lot to absorb, this family history that was different from what she'd grown up believing.

Tragedy is tragedy, she knew. But she wondered what else Grandma Josie had to say on the matter. She was sure she'd find out soon enough.

5

ALTHOUGH TO EVERYONE but Mac it was universally agreed that there shouldn't be tomato sauce in the chicken soup, Calista's mother added it in anyway. She was always doing things like that, doing things for Mac, even though he couldn't taste her cooking anymore.

Calista's father ate dinner with them every night, although he didn't actually *eat* dinner. Instead, he sat at the table, admiring Nora, or occasionally passing conversation through Calista. Unlike other ghosts, Mac and Grandma Josie hadn't forgotten any of their lives, at least not yet. Part of the reason, they thought, was because they were tethered to their house. They hadn't left the grounds since returning, and therefore, it sort of cemented their place. Every night, they got the chance to interact with their family, even if it was through Calista. They'd never gotten lost.

Calista wondered why they didn't cross over, but she came to realize they each had their reasons. Grandma Josie didn't want to leave before knowing what had happened to her daughter, and Mac had stayed to watch over the family. Eventually they'd move on, Calista supposed. But for now, she knew she was lucky to have them.

It made her feel special, being the only one who could hear her father and grandmother. But now Calista feared the moment it would be gone. Would she still be special? Would anything matter the same afterward?

"I think my tooth is growing," Molly said from across the table, grinning and pointing to the gap where a tooth was most definitely not growing. "Look, Mom," she said, opening her mouth wider. "Look!"

"Wow," Nora said. "That's amazing, Molly." Calista's mother shot her an amused look before taking a sip of her iced tea.

But Calista was having a hard time finding a smile. She kept thinking about the family curse. And then she felt selfish. There were children missing. Children hurt and worse. That should be her main concern.

Thomas had been in her room this morning and she'd brushed him aside. She knew it wasn't entirely her fault—he was the fifth boy to show up in her room this year. A few months ago, a kid from 1928 had appeared in a lavender shirt and small wire-rimmed glasses. He showed up while Calista was changing, and she chewed him out pretty thoroughly. Later, she discovered he'd been in an accident on his way to school, struck by a bus on her very street. The impact had knocked him straight out of his shoes. That was why he was there. One of his shoes was still missing. Once Calista helped him find it . . . well, the ghost disappeared. Moved on. He didn't even thank Calista for spending two whole days digging around in the mud at the base of the trees on her block.

But Thomas was different. She didn't know him, didn't recognize him from town, even though Meadowmere was so small. He might have been homeschooled. But now Calista worried that Thomas was looking for more than his mother. He might not even know it, but he might want Calista to find . . . to find his body. And then she'd have to find his killer.

She gulped. Why had her grandmother pointed her to that page in her books? What did any of this have to do with her family's curse other than the boys being thirteen? And, biggest question of all, why would someone be warning, or threatening, the Wynn family?

"Callie?" her mother called, sounding like she'd called a few times already. Startled, Calista looked over.

"What'd you say?" she asked, distracted.

"I said"—her mother smiled—"how was your day? Anything new?"

Calista looked down at her soup, slowly stirring it. She should tell her mother about the missing boys, at least. And about Molly seeing a ghost lady. It might even be good to bring up how left out she'd been feeling at school, or her fear surrounding her birthday. But she didn't want to worry her mother about any of those things.

Since Mac died, Calista's mother had been overwhelmed. They weren't the kind of family that had life insurance. Mac had made a little money on the side reading tarot or helping locals with small projects, but he lost his ability to communicate with the dead when he was thirteen, just like his living sisters. His main job was working construction for a parking lot company, building five-story garages. That was what happened to him. An accident from the fifth floor.

The company gave Calista's mother Mac's last paycheck and their condolences. A few of Mac's friends scraped together enough money to help pay for the funeral. After that, Nora had to make ends meet. She worked two jobs, one at the school cafeteria across town, and another on the weekends at the Five and Diner.

The family still made a little money reading tarot and helping out locals, but only the truly desperate came to Calista. And when they did, she usually didn't have the heart to charge them. She could have sold Grandma Josie's charms or artifacts from the séance room for extra cash, but nowadays, so few believed in the supernatural that the spells probably wouldn't have worked anyway.

The trick to success? Complete belief. That was the only way any of it would work.

"Everything all right?" Calista's mother asked her. "You're being incredibly quiet."

"Go on and tell her about the missing kids," Mac encouraged, leaning into the table. "She should know." Calista's father had a spot set out for him at every meal, just like Grandma Josie did. A table set for five. It would be tough to explain to her friends if they ever came over. If she had any friends.

Calista looked at her father, but ultimately, when she turned back to her mom, she found Nora's eyes tired from a long shift at work. Calista's heart sank just a little.

"It was a good day, Mom," she said. "How about you?"

Her mother smiled, clearly relieved. "Oh, my day?" she asked, turning toward Molly to give her a playful look. "Do you know what we had to cook for breakfast today?"

"What?" Molly asked, excited. She loved their mother's stories about work, mostly because Nora knew just the content to keep Molly entertained.

"I call it *monster mash*," she said, widening her eyes. "It was scrambled egg powder, sausages, and extra gooey green sliiiiiime!"

"Ewww . . . ," Molly yelled, laughing. Nora reached out to tickle Molly and her laughs filled the room with lightness, happiness.

Calista smiled and Mac laughed. It was joyful, and for a moment, it felt like old times. But when Calista glanced to the end of the table, she noticed Grandma Josie staring down at her hands knotted together in front of her.

Her grandmother looked worried. No, she looked . . . scared.

Calista wondered if the rest of her father's siblings had been as in the dark as he was about the Wynn family's past. She had two aunts in central New York, out near Syracuse. They ran a small curiosity antique shop together, the Sisters Charmed. Her uncle Modine lived somewhere in California, although he'd lost touch with the family before she was born, and her aunt Arabelle was in Buffalo raising her two sons.

Which left Aunt Freya. Although Grandma Josie always claimed she didn't have favorites, she had a close relationship with her oldest living daughter. Whenever they were in the same room together, unspoken words seemed to dance between the two women, even after Grandma Josie's death. Almost like . . . they had a secret.

With this new information about a family curse, Calista wondered if that was exactly what it was—a secret. She turned to her mother.

"Mom," Calista asked, drawing her mother's attention, "do you know if Aunt Freya is back in Louisiana yet?"

Her mother looked at the ceiling, thinking on it. "You know," she said, "I haven't heard from her in a couple weeks. You should call and see how she's doing. I know she had planned to come out for your thirteenth birthday."

Calista flinched at the mention. Her mother groaned softly, knowing how much Calista was dreading the date.

"Sorry," Nora murmured. "I didn't mean to . . . You know," she added, reaching out to grasp Calista's hand on the table. Her touch was warm and comforting. "You should talk with your aunt. I think it could help you," her mother said. "She *understands*."

What Freya understood was the loss of identity that Calista was about to endure. The loss of her family. She had once been a powerful medium, and Freya continued to radiate power even after her gift to speak to the dead left her. Despite that, she didn't practice magic anymore. No charms, no spells. She worked for a photography studio, although no one at her work quite knew how she was able to always get the perfect photo. It was because Freya could read minds a little. She knew just what to say to get the reaction she needed.

Before leaving to go back home after Mac's funeral, Freya had passed Calista a small book of poems that she said Mac had loved when he was a kid. She asked Calista to read them to him once in a while. Let him know that she was always thinking of him.

She was right. Although he didn't like to show it, Mac grieved his own death. The poems brought him some comfort in those times.

So, yeah. Aunt Freya understood loss.

But maybe she also understood a little bit more.

6

CALISTA'S MOTHER TUCKED Molly into bed after dinner, and then came back to the kitchen as Calista was finishing the dishes. Mac and Grandma Josie were in the basement, deciding on summoning spells for the missing boy Thomas. He hadn't tried to contact Calista since that morning, so they'd have to find him. They would need just the right spell. The wrong one, it turned out, could be dangerous.

"I'm heading to bed, honey," Nora told her daughter, fighting back a yawn.

Calista saw that her mother had a book in her hand and her reading glasses on her head. She wouldn't make it a chapter before drifting off to sleep. Nora always went to bed early, much earlier than Calista. She worked first shift at the school, just as the sun was coming up. Calista usually didn't mind. Her dad and grandmother were there to keep her company. But it could be a pain sometimes, especially if Molly was being difficult about getting ready.

But tonight, Molly went to bed without a fuss and Calista was grateful for that. She had big plans for tonight and her anxiety was climbing the later it got in the evening. Summoning spirits always made Calista uneasy. And in addition, this was possibly a murder. What would she discover when she talked to Thomas?

Nora came over to kiss the top of Calista's head. "Don't stay up too late," her mother told her before walking into the hallway.

Calista stayed at the sink, her hands in the warm dishwater, until she heard her mother's bedroom door close. Then Calista sighed and pulled the plug in the sink, the sound of draining water echoing in the room. She never had told her mother about the missing boys. She'd have to do that tomorrow, unless, of course, her mother heard about it first.

Grabbing a dish towel from the handle of the oven, Calista dried her hands and then hung the towel back up. She grabbed the plate of cookies she'd made earlier, a sweet treat for spirits, and then clicked off the light in the kitchen.

As she made her way to her bedroom with the plate, Calista had so much to consider. But she couldn't help another moment of guilt. Should she have at least told her mother that she was having a séance tonight? Ultimately, she'd decided not to. Her mother wasn't a medium. It would just worry her.

It worried Calista too. She'd summoned plenty of ghosts, at least a dozen. But every séance had a set of risks, things that could go wrong. Some of those possibilities were:

Nothing at all could happen and Calista
would have wasted an entire night and an
expensive set of candles

Technical difficulties: ghosts without voices,
apparitions that were too hard to see, flickering visions

More than one ghost could come through

Possession

It was the fourth possibility that terrified Calista. Possession was rare; ghosts definitely did *not* want to possess the
living, no matter how many horror movies showed the con-
trary. But there were a few documented cases.

In fact, it had happened once to Grandma Josie. She told
Calista the story shortly before she passed away, back when
Calista would sit with her to keep her company while she
was bedridden. Turned out, when Grandma Josie was a little girl, a spirit was so angry that he jumped right inside her
body during a séance with his wife. She didn't elaborate on
what happened, only that it took another medium to get him
out, a sort of exorcism for the gifted. After that, Grandma
Josie didn't do séances for strangers anymore, even as she
assured Calista they were safe.

"Those were different times," Grandma Josie had said.
"The dead don't get angry like that anymore. And besides,
your father and I will always make sure you only help the
good spirits."

Calista closed her bedroom door and set the plate on her dresser while she dragged the small round table she kept in the corner to the center of the room. In the basement, the family had an official séance room, a room where they met with their clients. It was burgundy and gold, ornate in a way that made people feel both comfortable and untethered. A room where it felt like anything was possible. But it wasn't necessary to have a place like that to call up spirits. It was just part of the show.

It would be too obvious if Calista went into the basement tonight. She'd have to make do in her room. Calista gathered the candles she needed from her dresser and placed them on the table, lighting each one at a slow and determined pace. Her father and grandmother appeared in the room, and Calista brought over chairs for them on either side of her, leaving an empty seat for Thomas.

"Now listen close," Grandma Josie said, coming to stand next to Calista. "You're going to use configuration four."

"Four?" Calista asked, turning to her. "Isn't that too restrictive?"

"It's for your protection," Grandma Josie said curtly, and instructed her to begin drawing.

Although confused, Calista did as she was told. She grabbed a piece of chalk and drew a circle in the center of the table, an earlier design having faded since the last time she'd done this. It'd been at least three months since she'd called on the boy with the missing shoe, maybe a little longer. She hoped this summoning would be as simple, as safe. But she had a feeling that the chances of that were pretty unlikely. She hated the selfish thought—a boy had been murdered, after all. There was no room for fear when doing what was right.

The configuration was intricate, and although she knew it, Calista had never used it before. There were several points, complicated loops. It took her three tries to get the proportions right. When she was done, Calista grabbed the plate of cookies and set it in the middle of the table.

Once everything was arranged, and Mac and Grandma Josie were situated, Calista turned out the light and took her seat.

In a low voice, Grandma Josie told her which moves to make with her fingers, which words to use. Calista listened closely, trying not to overthink the instructions; otherwise it could dilute her intent and prevent the spirits from seeing her.

Because really, that was what she looked like to spirits from the other side. A bright beacon of light, the kind to draw moths to a flame. Calista knew she was about to be shining. But as her grandmother spoke, Calista realized this summoning spell was different. Normally her presence was an open window for spirits to climb through. But with Grandma Josie's spell, her presence became a pinhole, designed to only let in the spirit specified. That would make summoning more difficult, but Calista was sure her grandmother had her reasons.

As she sat there, ready to start, Calista could feel the warmth from the flickering candles on her cheeks. She looked over and saw that Grandma Josie was twisting her hands on the table, a nervous fidget she'd never quite gotten over. Mac noticed and reached to put his hand over his mother's to steady her. Then, Mac turned to smile at Calista, encouraging her to begin. Calista set her palms flat on the table, took a deep breath, and closed her eyes.

"Our beloved Thomas Hassel, we bring you gifts from life into death. Commune with us, Thomas, and move among us," Calista said. She then spoke the words in Latin that her grandmother had taught her, every syllable said with confidence. Power.

When she finished, Calista felt a cool breeze move past her, and the candles' lights flickered under the pressure. She opened her eyes.

"Hi, Thomas," she said kindly to the boy sitting across from her.

"Hello," he said with a smile, and his voice echoed, wispy and faraway. His presence was different now, mostly controlled but also more distant due to the summoning spell. But it was the clearest way to talk to him. When spirits just show up, they can't always control how long they're visible. Right now, Thomas was tethered to her.

"Are you going to help me?" the boy asked hopefully.

"I'm going to try," Calista replied. "And maybe you'll be able to help me, too. Should we get started?"

He nodded emphatically. "I'd like to see my mother," he rushed to say. "I want my mom."

Calista saw her father wince while Grandma Josie kept her gaze on the table. Working with ghosts was often heartbreaking work. Calista let the painful sentiment slide off her, though. She had to stay calm. Any flash of emotion could cut the summoning short, severing the tie between the veils.

"Do you remember your mom, Thomas?" Calista asked. His smiled faded, and he knitted his eyebrows together.

"Yes, she . . ." he started, but his concentration trailed off. Calista could see that he was having trouble remembering. She adjusted her posture and pressed on.

"What does she look like?" Calista asked. If she helped him call up details, it might trigger his memory. She'd start with his mother and move on from there.

"Oh," he said, thinking it over. "My mom is very pretty. She has . . . she has brown hair. No, it was red, right?" he asked, unsure.

Calista had no idea what his mother looked like, but she nodded for him to continue, watching his expression as the memories of his life slowly filled in.

"Yes, curly red hair," he said. "But . . . but I always looked like my dad."

"And do you remember the last time you saw your parents?" Calista asked.

"Uh . . ." He looked flustered, and Calista backed up, trying not to make him uncomfortable. An uncomfortable spirit was an unruly spirit. Summoning was all about keeping control of the room.

"Do you have any brothers or sisters?" Calista asked lightly, changing the topic. Thomas thought for a moment, and then nodded.

"Yes," he said. "I have two little brothers." He smiled at the thought of them. Calista felt another tug on her heart. No doubt Thomas's little brothers were missing him right now.

"What are their names?" Calista asked.

"Anthony and Michael," he said. "Anthony . . . He's going to be in sixth grade next year."

His memories were coming more clearly, and Calista leaned forward slightly, careful not to lift her hands from the table. She let Thomas discuss his brothers, his mother, and his friends. The memories were filling out and it felt like progress. His spirit had grown very clear, very present.

When he seemed to run out of things to say, Calista focused her questions, getting closer to the answers she hoped to find. The news report said that Thomas had disappeared from his bedroom. She needed to get him there.

"And your bedroom?" Calista asked. "Can you describe your room?"

"It's small," he said, thinking on it. "Really small. But I have posters on my walls, a desk to do my homework and my own TV." He smiled. "That's where I play video games. And—"

Thomas stopped abruptly. He was already very pale—he was dead, after all—but Calista saw what little color he had left drain away. Calista's heart rate sped up.

"And *what*, Thomas?" she asked. "What happened in your room? Where did you go?"

His lower lip quivered and his blue eyes filled with tears. "I . . . I saw her," he whispered.

Calista felt a wave of sickness, her stomach churning. The temperature in the room began to drop, her breath becoming white puffs in the air. She wanted to look at her father, but she couldn't turn her gaze away from Thomas. He was desperate. Frightened. She couldn't look away and risk losing him.

"Tell me who you saw," Calista said. "What happened to you, Thomas?"

"I can't," he mouthed, his eyes growing very wide.

Slowly, his gaze lifted to something above Calista's shoulder. In that moment, Calista felt as if there were icy fingers on the back of her neck. And yet, she couldn't look away from Thomas.

"What do you see?" she asked him, having to work hard to keep the shaking from her voice. "W-What's behind me?"

Suddenly, Thomas slapped both of his palms over his eyes. The temperature in the room plummeted, and a gust of wind blew the candles out, submerging the room in darkness. Calista gasped, and, knowing it might end the séance, she lifted her hands from the table to find the box of matches. She fumbled with them, and Mac whispered, "Stay calm, Callie. Stay calm."

Finally, Calista struck the match along the box and lit it. A perfect circle of light formed around the fire she was holding. She lifted her gaze to where Thomas was sitting, but the moment she did, a woman's face appeared just inches from hers.

The woman was pale and very, very dead.

Calista screamed, dropping the match. It sizzled out on the table, leaving her in darkness once again. For a moment, Calista couldn't catch her breath, as if the woman had snatched it from her lungs.

"It's her," Grandma Josie murmured in the most terrified voice Calista had ever heard her use. The sound of it scared her more than anything else.

Calista picked up the matches again. When she lit one, she was relieved that the woman was no longer in front of her. With her hands still shaking, Calista touched the flame to the candle wick, illuminating the room. But what she saw did not comfort her.

She looked across the table toward Thomas and found

him stiff and immobile, his eyes unnaturally wide and his head tipped back. Standing behind him was the woman—the Tall Lady, Calista guessed. The woman was wearing a yellow gown, her dark hair tied up in knots with unruly pieces hanging around her face, her lips bloodred. She stood behind Thomas with her hand on his cheek, her long black nails pressing on his skin. The woman stared directly at Calista, and despite all the questions she had, Calista found herself unable to speak.

The Tall Lady radiated terror. She oozed malice. Calista tried to catch her breath, and just as she was about to speak, the Tall Lady silenced her with a devilish smile, her teeth tiny and misplaced—sharpened. Calista's heart was pumping so hard it made her ears hurt.

Very slowly, the Tall Lady pursed her red lips and murmured, "Limbus . . ."

And then, in a flurry of movement, her fingernails slashed across Thomas's face and the boy burst into a cloud of black ash. Calista screamed again, jumping up from her chair.

The Tall Lady disappeared as the ashes of Thomas continued to fall throughout the room like snow.

"No!" Calista cried, rushing forward as if she could catch them. Instead, the ashes coated her hands in black soot. The boy was long gone. Lost.

Calista's bedroom door burst open as her mother frantically rushed inside. Nora paused, stunned, before reaching to flick on the overhead lights.

"Callie, what in the world?" she muttered. But her mother couldn't ask anything else, staring around the room at the ashes still in the air. Nora looked at her daughter, but Calista stood frozen, scared.

After another moment, Calista turned toward her father, who seemed just as utterly shocked. Grandma Josie watched in horrified silence as the boy's ashes fell. And then Calista turned, ran into her mother's arms, and sobbed.

7

CALISTA SAT ON the floor of her room, her entire body shaking. The air still smelled of burnt toast and melted candle wax. Moonlight streamed in the window with the curtains open as Calista continued to sort through her thoughts. Nora was unhappy that Calista had had a late-night séance in her room, but eventually, after Calista calmed, her mother helped her clean up.

Calista gave her mother the barest of details—a boy had appeared to her this morning and she was trying to help him. But something went wrong with the summoning and his spirit . . . exploded.

But in truth, Calista still wasn't sure what had happened. She had no idea what it meant, for her or for Thomas. All she knew was that she was terrified. And she needed to talk to her father and grandmother to figure it out before alarming her mother.

When the ashes had been swept up and new sheets placed

on the bed, Nora paused at the doorway, her face still a portrait of concern.

"You sure you don't want to sleep in my bed tonight?" she asked. "There's plenty of room."

"Thanks, but I'm fine," Calista told her. "Plus, I need to do a little studying. I have a test in math tomorrow." Which was true, although she wasn't going to study tonight.

"Okay," Nora said, still a little reluctant. "Well, promise me you'll wake me if anything else strange happens. Or if you get nervous. Anything at all."

"I promise," Calista told her, placing her hand over her heart. Her mother smiled at her lovingly.

"See you in the morning," she said, although that wasn't entirely true. Her mother was usually off to work before she woke.

Calista waited until her mother left, and when she was gone, she went over to sit on her freshly made bed. Her posture sagged as she thought about Thomas.

"Are you all right, kiddo?" Mac asked. He stood over his daughter, his dark eyes searching her face as he took stock of her condition. He held out his hand to her from habit, although if she reached for it, Calista knew she wouldn't find any comfort there.

Something that felt extra unfair in that moment. Especially since random ghosts had been able to touch Calista in the past. But for some reason, the people she wanted to hug most right now were out of her reach.

Mac glanced down at his own hand, frowning at how useless it seemed, and sat next to Calista on the bed. She turned to him, tears springing to her eyes.

"Is Thomas gone?" she asked. "Is he gone for good?"

"I'm not sure," Mac said. "I've never . . . I've never seen anything like that." He turned to look at Grandma Josie. "Have you, Mom?" he asked. Grandma Josie sat in the chair at the corner of the room, the table and other chairs from the séance put back in their spots.

Grandma Josie didn't answer right away; she didn't even lift her head.

There was a soft knock at the door, and Calista and her father turned that way.

"Yes?" Calista called quietly. The door opened slowly, the hinges creaking and dragging out the mystery. "Hello?" Calista said into the darkness of the hallway. Just then, Molly appeared, walking into the room and rubbing her sleepy eyes.

"Callie?" she asked. "What are you doing?"

This made Calista jump to her feet. She met Molly near the door and turned her sister back toward her room, ready to send her into the hallway. "What are you doing up?" she asked Molly. "You have school in the morning."

"I came to tell you to stop," Molly said, her voice still sleepy.

"What are you talking about?" Calista asked. "Stop what?"

"I don't know," Molly said. "But the Tall Lady was in

my room. And she told me to tell you to stop. Stop because you've made her mad."

Calista's stomach dropped. She turned back toward her father, her eyes wide and fearful, then she looked down at her sister. She put her hand protectively on Molly's shoulder. "The Tall Lady was in your room?" she asked her.

"Yes," Molly said. "And she was very mad, Callie. She's not the same when she's mad. I didn't like it."

"The next time she comes to you, you find me, all right?" Calista said. "Don't talk to her anymore—you find me. Promise?"

"I promise," Molly agreed, blinking slowly. She was still half asleep. Calista wondered if she should bring her sister to their mother's room, but ultimately, the house felt warm and spirit-free. She could tell that the danger had passed. At least for now.

But just in case, Calista led Molly back to bed in her pink-painted room, moving over her stuffed animals as she tucked her in.

"I'm cold," Molly murmured. "Can I have another blanket?"

Calista grabbed one from the chair in the corner of her room and laid it over her sister, brushing her hair back from her face. She wasn't running a fever and the room temperature felt fine. But she didn't want the little girl to be cold.

Molly's eyes slid shut the moment she settled into her pillow.

Before leaving the room, Calista looked around, checking

for signs of the Tall Lady lingering. She didn't feel any negative presence. The room was clear. She stayed a moment longer before reluctantly leaving.

Calista returned to her room to talk to her father and grandmother. Mac was still sitting on the bed, but Grandma Josie was pacing, casting impatient glances out the window. Calista eased the bedroom door shut.

"I got Molly to sleep," she said. "But what happened during the séance? Have you ever experienced anything like that before?" Calista was still shaken, traumatized by the fear in Thomas's eyes before he had been turned to ash.

"No," Mac replied, shaking his head. "Never. And I've got to be honest, Callie. I don't want you or Molly near this Tall Lady. She's not like other spirits."

Calista was surprised by her father's reaction. "I can't just stop," she said. "The Tall Lady is contacting Molly. We have to figure out who she is and what she wants. And I have an idea. I think I should summon the other missing boy— Devon Winters."

"No," Mac said, getting to his feet. "We don't know enough to call to his spirit. Look, I know you're strong, Callie, but that spirit—she's powerful. She walked right through your grandmother's configuration. If she comes back, I'm not sure you're equipped to handle her."

"But what if I'm the only one who can help?" Calista asked.

"I need you to stay away from that woman," Mac replied, more insistent.

"Trust me, I'd love to," Calista said. "But she—"

"I know her," Grandma Josie announced abruptly.

Both Calista and Mac stopped talking and turned toward the old woman. Grandma Josie stood at the bedroom window, staring out into the darkness.

"You . . . do?" Calista asked, stunned. "Why didn't you say something earlier? Who is she? How can we stop her?"

"Her name was Edwina Swift," Grandma Josie said. Her voice was quiet, but after a moment, she walked back over to settle into the chair, moving slowly even though ghosts didn't have achy bones. A leftover habit from life, Calista supposed. "She and I grew up in this town," Grandma Josie continued. "Edwina was a few years older than me. Her family owned a house and a small bit of land out near the marshes. But they died when she was a teenager."

"Near the marshes?" Calista asked, confused. "But there's nothing there."

"Not anymore," Grandma Josie said. "The ground sucked it up, sucked her little shack right into the mud where it belonged. It was . . ." She closed her eyes. "It was where my daughter died."

Calista froze in shock. Grandma Josie's earlier secret began to make more sense. There was more to the story of Aunt Virginia's death that Grandma Josie hadn't shared. So what exactly happened all those years ago?

"You're talking about Virginia?" Mac asked, taking a step toward her. "Mom, are you saying the spirit who showed up tonight had something to do with my sister's death?"

"It wasn't just your sister," Grandma Josie said. "You were young then, Mac. You didn't know what was what. Your father had passed, passed right through and didn't come back. We were mourning. But then, several children in Meadowmere went missing."

The true gravity of the situation finally clicked together for Calista. "This has happened before . . . ," she whispered.

Grandma Josie nodded, her face stricken with grief. "I tried to help back then. The sheriff came to me personally—his boy Davey was one of the missing. And as I searched, all the clues pointed me toward Edwina. She'd been a powerful medium. A rival, I suppose. But she dealt in dark spells, the sort of things I would never fool with. The sort of magic that required . . . sacrifice. I knew then that those children were long gone."

Calista's grandmother detested any supernatural spells or communications that were pulled through using anguish or anger. She'd told her granddaughter that emotions needed to be set aside to keep a medium from clouding their purpose. Anger and fear invited demons. Scary things. Things that could hurt.

"One night I summoned little Davey's spirit," Grandma Josie continued. "And he pointed me toward the marshes in Edwina's yard. Said he drowned there with the others. When I reported it to the sheriff, he went out there with a mob of people. They all knew of Edwina's reputation. I thought I had done the right thing reporting her, but . . ." Grandma Josie's voice trailed off and she looked out the window again. "The town decided to exact its own justice. There was no arrest. No questions. No trial. They murdered Edwina in her home in the dead of night, a big crowd surrounding her shack."

Calista's heart beat wildly. The town murdered Edwina, outside the lines of justice. That sort of thing . . . it wouldn't have ended well for a new spirit. Especially not a spirit with dark magic.

"That very next night," Grandma Josie said, her voice pitched low, "I heard a racket in Virginia's room. My daughter was at the park with her friends, so I went to check what it could be. But when I opened her bedroom door, I found Edwina standing there, her yellow dress billowing around her. She was very much dead. Very much angry. She smiled and told me I'd pay for my role in her murder. Said we'd all pay."

Calista's father was breathing quickly, his eyes rounded in horror. Calista wished she could take his hand to comfort him. Virginia had been his sister. Calista understood how strong the bond between siblings could be, especially in a family of mediums.

Grandma Josie swallowed hard, her face crumpling before she spoke again. "It was a few nights later when Virginia went missing. The night of her birthday," Grandma Josie said in a cracked voice. "I told everyone that Edwina had been involved, but she was dead. They thought I'd lost my mind. But . . . they did eventually find my baby. They found her inside Edwina's old shack, the phrase 'thirteen by thirteen' written in ash on the table. 'The child had a weak heart,' the sheriff wrote in his report. A heart attack at thirteen years old? Shame on him. Shame on all of them."

"How could they have known?" Calista asked, trying to offer an explanation.

"Because they lived in this town, too," Grandma Josie said. "These people have always known who we are, Calista. They've always known we were mediums. They knew what Edwina was enough to fear her. But they conveniently forgot it once she was dead. Once it was *my* child missing. Over the years, the sheriff retired and passed on. A lot of the other families moved upstate. Edwina was forgotten. The marsh reclaimed her land, her home, and she was erased. I can't say I wasn't happy to see her gone. Gone for good, I'd hoped. But her curse showed the next year when Freya lost her gift. And it continued down the line, the curse of thirteen. And now . . . she's back," Grandma Josie said, shaking her head. "And I'm scared. I'm scared she's coming for another Wynn girl."

Calista shuddered with fear. "She's coming . . . on my thirteenth birthday?" she asked, frightened.

"I don't think it's you that she wants," Grandma Josie replied. "I'm not trying to scare you, but if she wanted you, she would have taken you by surprise. No, this is something more. She wants revenge. Not just on us, but on the whole town. You need to stop her."

"I want to!" Calista said with a surge of desperation. "But how do I beat someone like her? She just destroyed Thomas with the slash of her hand. And she hides from me—she won't even let me see her."

"The poor boy is gone now," Grandma Josie said, tears dripping onto her wrinkled cheeks. "Edwina trapped his spirit with the others, I assume. And . . . and I don't know how to win against her," Grandma Josie admitted. "I never did. Edwina is a wicked woman, a danger to us all. Her curse was just the beginning. She won't rest until we're all dead and forgotten, like her. She'll start with us and then she'll take the entire town."

Calista couldn't let that happen. She straightened her posture.

"Then I'll stop her," she said, trying to sound brave. But deep down, she knew beating a powerful medium was close to impossible, especially when she had less than a week left with her full gifts.

She'd have to think faster. Her father was right—she couldn't do this alone. Calista would need help and she knew just who to ask.

"It's time to call Aunt Freya," Calista said.

Mac looked over with a flash of relief. Grandma Josie

pressed her lips together firmly, as if agreeing.

Aunt Freya will know what to do, Calista thought. *She always has the answers.*

Calista got her phone out of her backpack, the battery signaling that it was low. It was an outdated model, her father's old phone, and she plugged it in. Impatiently, Calista found her aunt's number and pressed call.

She held her breath as it rang, unsure of where to even start. It was on the third ring when it picked up.

"My, my," Freya said, with a soft Southern accent from her years in Louisiana. On the other end of the phone line, Calista could hear music, the chatter of people. "It's been a minute since I heard from you, Calista Wynn. How have you been, my darling girl?"

Calista smiled. Her aunt always made her feel loved, special. "Aunt Freya," she said, "I'm sorry to call you out of the blue, but something is happening in Meadowmere. I . . . We need you. Can you talk?"

Calista was met with silence mixed with the murmur of music and voices in the background. When her aunt spoke again, her voice sounded closer, as though her lips were pressed to the receiver.

"Is that what I've been feeling?" Freya asked. "I thought maybe it was just another Wynn losing her gift, but it's more, isn't it?"

"A lot more," Calista replied, nodding even though her aunt couldn't see her.

"Mm-hmm," Freya said. "And is my mother there with you? Your father?"

"They're both here," Calista said.

"And they let you call me? Oh, dear." She waited a long moment. "Tell you what," Freya said. "You hang tight, go about your business, your real-life business. I'll catch a bus once I'm done here—should be there for your birthday. Can you wait that long?"

"I . . . I'm not sure," she told her honestly. "Kids are going missing."

"Then I'll be there in two days," Freya said abruptly. "I'll catch a flight, but I have something here I have to deal with first. You wait for me. Whatever this is," she added, "you keep it quiet, understand? We can't trust the people in town, not with the big secrets. You grasp what I mean by that, right? We don't need their kind of . . . justice."

So Freya knew about Edwina and the town's vigilantes. Could something like that happen again? If people in town were looking to lay blame about missing kids, would they point to the only mediums left? That possibility was terrifying.

"I'll wait for you," Calista said. She needed Freya now, but until she arrived, Calista would just have to keep a close eye on her sister. She wasn't going to let anything happen to Molly.

"Good girl," Freya told her. "Now, you stay strong. They need you more than ever."

"I understand," Calista said, pushing away her fear. She

was the only Wynn left with the ability to contact the other side of the veil. "Thank you, Aunt Freya."

"Of course," she replied. "Now give the others my best and I'll see you soon."

And with that, Freya hung up, leaving Calista hopeful that she'd be able to help. Her aunt would be there soon, but in the meantime, Calista was going to put together her own spell to protect the house. She would use configuration eight, the strongest protection spell she knew. Even stronger than what Grandma Josie used earlier during the séance.

Configuration eight included small charms—bits of copper, wood, and sprinkles of moon water that had been left out in the light of a full moon to charge. It was a complicated configuration, so Calista asked her father for help with the drawing. She marked the entry to the house with chalk, just under the rug so her mother wouldn't notice. As she did this, she concentrated on the Tall Lady, etching the name Edwina into a space near the exit. She wasn't welcome in their house.

After walking the entire house, leaving coins and bits of wood in the corners, and sealing it all up with the moon water, Calista let out a grateful sigh. She was sure that the house felt warmer somehow. Pulsing with protection. With love.

They were safe tonight, she felt. And hopefully her aunt would be there soon to help them figure out the rest.

8

IT SEEMED LITERALLY impossible that Calista had to get her sister ready for school, eat breakfast, and walk her to the bus the day after she had watched a ghost get murdered in her bedroom. And yes, she realized the strangeness in even having that thought. Up until last night, Calista hadn't even known that ghosts could get murdered—they were already dead.

Calista had had a hard time sleeping. The image of Thomas turning into ash was at the front of her mind. She felt horrible for him. She wished she could have stopped what was happening, helped him somehow. But Grandma Josie had told her long ago that she couldn't take responsibility for the spirits. There were too many and life was too short. So Calista grieved him quietly and hoped that once she found answers, it would offer all of them some comfort.

Calista walked along the hall of Kennedy Middle School, keeping her head down as other students passed, occupied with their own conversations. Jill Haddock was getting her braces off next week and she was secretly worried her teeth would still be crooked. Marisol Hernandez was wondering what she should get her mother for her birthday. And Amen Wallace knew he'd make the varsity basketball team when he got to high school next year. He was that good.

All these thoughts and words swirled around Calista, bits of conversation, pieces of emotion radiating off her classmates. Her senses felt sharper today; even the ever-present smell of tater tots from the cafeteria and the quiet buzz that was always humming from the overhead loudspeaker seemed clearer. It was all very distracting.

Calista hiked her backpack onto her shoulders as she entered her math class. The room was bare compared to the other classrooms. Her math teacher thought posters and bright colors were a distraction. Calista knew that if Mrs. Carlo could black out the windows to keep them from daydreaming, she would.

Calista took her seat toward the back of the room, easing into her chair and setting her backpack at her feet. Calista took out her green notebook—the one with the edges curled from being jammed into her pack next to the heavy math textbook. Once, on television, Calista had watched a show where all the students had laptop computers at their desks, reading their textbooks online. Not at Kennedy. They didn't even have the budget to keep the playground from sinking into the mud.

Mrs. Carlo hadn't arrived yet, so Calista used the moment to stare out the window at the dying grass and think about the Tall Lady. The other students in the room were chatting, getting louder as the time for the bell grew closer. An excited energy pulsed at the possibility of their teacher showing up late. Mrs. Carlo rarely did anything out of the ordinary.

As she stared out the window, watching a bird peck at the wood of an old, twisted tree, Calista tried to picture the Tall Lady as a person, as Edwina—a woman living in her shack in the marshes. But the woman Calista saw in her bedroom seemed like she'd always been dead. There was no life in her eyes, only malice and cruelty. Death.

No, Calista couldn't imagine the Tall Lady had ever been real at all. However, she knew that her aunt Virginia was well-loved by her family. She'd heard her father talk about losing his sister and how the trauma of it was imprinted on their entire family. Sometimes, Calista could feel the grief as if it seeped down from the previous generation—sadness as a hereditary condition.

She'd seen pictures of Virginia, but they all seemed so old-fashioned, out of time and out of place. There was one picture where Virginia was holding a puppy, a rottweiler she'd rescued from the marshes. She was laughing with shining brown eyes. Just a year after that smiling photo, Virginia was gone.

"Hey," a voice whispered, startling Calista out of her head. She turned quickly, her heart pounding, and was surprised to find Wyland Davis squatting next to her desk.

Calista couldn't respond at first. She was surprised to be so close to anyone who wasn't her family. Most kids never got that near to her, kept back by an invisible barrier. Wyland wasn't held in the same way, and it was just . . . It was strange.

"You okay?" Wyland asked, his dark brows knitted together. "Am I bothering you?"

Calista's mouth opened and then closed as she thought and then rethought her response. No, he wasn't bothering her. She studied him a moment. Wyland had unruly dark hair, dark eyes, and dark freckles on soft brown skin. He had a combination of features that Calista found fascinating, although she'd admit she'd never really noticed before then.

"It's fine," she managed to say, and readjusted in her seat, laying her palms flat on the desk as if grounding herself, just like she'd ground a spirit during a séance. Keep them from suddenly disappearing.

Wyland shot a nervous look at the door, as if expecting Mrs. Carlo at any moment. He turned back to Calista and leaned in to whisper. "I don't mean to put you on the spot," he said quietly, "but I heard you . . . *you know things*. Is that true?"

For an instant, Calista wanted to deny it. But what would that accomplish? She *did* know things. It was an open secret throughout the community. Calista nodded, darting her eyes around the room to make sure the other kids weren't listening. But they were all absorbed in their own conversations, giggling and chatting outside of her bubble.

However, she realized that she could feel something—almost like a black cloud hovering over Wyland. Only she couldn't decipher what it meant, not without touching him and digging deeper. Did she really want to do that? Before she could decide, Wyland smiled.

"Cool," Wyland replied. "You see, there's this girl . . . and she—"

Calista felt her insides sink, her spike of adrenaline crashing hard enough to make her mouth dry, her eyes itch. Wyland was asking whether Moira Grace liked him, a fact that was not only obvious, but also so small in terms of what she did as a medium that Calista couldn't help but feel offended. She had summoned the spirit of a murdered boy last night. She wasn't here to play matchmaker.

Wyland must have realized her annoyance, because he abruptly stopped talking. His cheeks darkened with embarrassment, blotchy coloring crawling down his neck.

"Never mind," he said quickly, shaking his head. "I'm sorry, that was . . . Wow." He laughed, scratching at his hair. "That was wrong. I shouldn't have . . . I'm going back to my seat now." He tapped his knuckles on her desk as he climbed to his feet and headed across the room. He oozed embarrassment, the wave so intense that Calista felt sympathetic. She should have indulged him a little.

Wyland Davis had wondered if Moira liked him after getting several anonymous texts telling him he was cute. But he didn't want to risk the humiliation of asking if it was her in case it wasn't. He needn't worry. Moira and her friend Casey, who also liked Wyland, had been sending those texts for weeks. They were building up the courage to tell him in person. They were almost there.

Still, Calista smiled a little. Wyland's vulnerability was endearing. So what explained the dark cloud she'd felt a moment ago, the cloud she *still* felt surrounding him? She lowered her head, closing her eyes as she tried to sort through the feeling. Maybe Wyland just really, *really* liked Moira? In that case, Calista could tell him about a love charm her grandmother had taught her when she was Molly's age. It didn't actually make anyone fall in love, that would be unethical. But clients felt more assured thinking they'd been given the real thing. Along with each charm, the new owner was given esteem-boosting words to repeat. That kind of positive self-talk worked wonders when trying to find the confidence to connect with other people.

Mrs. Carlo strode briskly into the classroom just as the late bell rang. She plopped her tote bag on her desk. Along with her came an aura of danger that Calista could sense but not understand. Mrs. Carlo was a mess; her blond hair ponytail had flyaways around her temples, and her glasses were askew. She adjusted them and began wringing her hands.

"Students," she said. "There's been . . . ah . . ." She fumbled with her words and looked helplessly at the doorway. "Principal Eagan will be in shortly to speak with you," she added. "You . . . You can open your books to chapter seven."

They'd already read chapter seven yesterday, but none of the class spoke up to remind her. She looked so rattled. Mrs. Carlo pulled out her desk chair and sat down on the edge of her seat, impatient and nervous.

The conversation and giggles had stopped the moment Mrs. Carlo walked in, and now they were replaced with concerned murmurs. Calista didn't have to be psychic to see that something was wrong. Calista turned and locked eyes with Wyland across the room. He nodded toward the front as if asking her if she knew what the situation was about. Calista shrugged, having no clear idea. It was too loud in the room, with too many competing emotions for her to focus on her teacher.

Mrs. Carlo continued to fret from her desk until Principal Eagan strode into the room with a uniformed officer at his side. Calista's eyes widened, a shot of fear racing through her system. This was definitely serious.

The two men scanned the room, but when Principal Eagan noticed Wyland, he adverted his eyes. Calista turned to him sharply and saw that Wyland had noticed it too. He swallowed hard.

"Students," Principal Eagan said to the room, "we have a situation. In light of recent events, we are in the process of contacting your parents and arranging transportation for you to leave for the day. We—"

"What?" McKayla Jardice said loudly, looking around. "What events? What's happening?"

Just then, students' phones around the classroom began to buzz and ring. Calista was tempted to check her phone to see if her mother was trying to get in touch with her, too. But the principal held up his hands.

"You'll all be able to call your parents in a moment," he announced, trying to calm the rising panic.

But the room was quickly devolving into chaos. The dark cloud wasn't just hovering over Wyland anymore. It was above all of them—hanging in the air like a storm brewing in the room.

Police sirens sounded in the distance, and as they grew louder, Calista knew they were coming toward the school. Just then, she felt a pull. She turned toward Wyland again and found him already staring at her.

And suddenly, the room around them seemed to fall away. Standing just behind Wyland's shoulder was a grainy apparition. And as she came into focus, the Tall Lady smiled, flashing her sharp teeth. She reached out her long nails, ready to scrape them along Wyland's flesh.

Calista jumped up from her chair in a burst of terror. "Leave him alone!" she yelled, pointing at Wyland.

In response, Wyland pushed back in his seat, alarmed by Calista's shout. The other kids in the class turned to look at them, both curious and frightened. To everyone else, Wyland was alone.

"Can someone *please* tell me what's going on?" McKayla called out, exasperated.

Calista looked at her, and when she turned back to Wyland, the Tall Lady was gone. Even in her absence, Wyland shivered, rubbing his upper arms to warm himself. His eyes were still searching Calista's face, trying to figure out what was happening.

"Please sit down, Calista," Principal Eagan said, casting a wary glance in her direction. He seemed to debate scolding her, and Calista wondered if it had something to do with her gifts. But then the principal turned to Wyland. "Mr. Davis," he added, dropping the tone of his voice, "we need to speak with you outside. Can you come with us?"

"No," Wyland said weakly. It wasn't defiant, it was scared. Calista could sense that he knew that the Tall Lady, or at least *something*, had been behind him a moment ago. Rather than argue, the principal grew somber. He nodded.

"The police are on their way, Wyland," he said, losing his formality. "It's . . . It's about your brother."

There were several gasps around the room. Calista's own breathing was becoming labored, uneven. The cloud above the room darkened even more.

"My brother?" Wyland asked, shocked. "This is about Parker?"

"He was in the front office a short while ago," the principal said. "He told Mrs. Rios that he had a message for you. When she called your mother, asking how Parker got here, your mother was understandably shocked. Your little brother had walked all the way from the elementary school without telling anyone. And then . . ." Principal Eagan rubbed nervously at his forehead. "He . . . He said something to Mrs. Rios, and she rushed to get me. But when we came back, Parker was gone. And no one has been able to find him since. He . . . He disappeared."

A fourth kid has gone missing, Calista thought. But she was startled, because it wasn't *her* thought. Like her aunt Freya, Calista could read minds sometimes. This was a bit different, though. It was . . . in her own voice. But Calista didn't understand what the words meant. As far as she knew, only Devon and Thomas had unknown whereabouts. Parker made three. Who was the fourth kid?

"Who else has gone missing?" Calista asked, earning a sharp look from the officer standing next to the principal. "There are four missing. Who else?"

"I said no such thing," Principal Eagan responded, loosening his tie as if it was suddenly too tight. True that he hadn't said it, but Calista had heard it nevertheless. "Please don't start rumors, Calista," the principal added before turning away.

Mrs. Carlo looked up from her desk. She eyed Calista carefully. She knew about Calista's family, although they had never spoken about it.

Four years ago, when Calista was only eight, Mrs. Carlo and her sister had come to the house to speak with Mac. Although Calista's father didn't talk to the dead, he still knew things. He suggested letting Calista help, but Mrs.

Carlo had turned down the offer. She didn't feel comfortable discussing her personal life in front of a child. Calista never did hear what their meeting was about; Mac always kept his clients' privacy.

Calista's principal cleared his throat and focused again on Wyland. Several students were already on their phones, talking worriedly to their parents. The sirens were louder now, but Calista tuned in to the conversation across the room.

"Are you sure you haven't heard from Parker?" Principal Eagan asked Wyland. "A text or call?"

Wyland took out his phone to check. "No," he said, absolutely miserable. "What did he . . . What did my brother come to tell me?"

The principal swallowed hard. "The message he gave Mrs. Rios was, 'Come and find me,'" Principal Eagan said.

Wyland winced, the words terrifying but also sad. His brother needed help.

Calista had no doubt, especially not after seeing her in the classroom. The Tall Lady had Parker.

Come and find me? Calista wasn't sure if the message was truly for Wyland. Or if it was intended for her to overhear.

Just then, Wyland looked over at Calista, tears brimming in his dark eyes. "Calista," he said, his voice low. "You have to help. You have to find my brother."

9

WYLAND HAD BEEN ushered out of the room before Calista got another chance to talk to him. His words stuck to her, though. His plea for help. There was so much emotional feedback going around that Calista was starting to feel sick to her stomach. There were panicked students, worried parents. So much chaos that she literally put her palms over her ears as she walked out of the building to head home.

Several cop cars were parked in the pick-up lane and a fire truck was at the curb in the teacher's lot. But no one had seen or heard from Parker Davis since he left the front office of Kennedy Middle School.

Calista had talked briefly on the phone to her mother, mostly to check on her little sister, who didn't have her own phone. Calista was relieved that her mother planned to leave early from work to pick up Molly from school. The elementary release was delayed until all parents could be contacted, so Nora offered to grab Calista on the way, but

Calista didn't want to burden her mother with the extra trip. She also didn't want to have to explain anything. Wyland had asked for her help, and she couldn't figure out how to give it with her mother fussing over her.

As Calista walked home, downtown Meadowmere was busier than it had been that morning. It was buzzing with frantic energy. There were adults gathered around, everyone talking, swapping stories and rumors. Calista listened as best as she could, but she also felt the stares of people as she passed. When Mrs. Gladys Winchell walked by, Calista felt a sharp poke of judgment. So sharp that she flinched.

She couldn't help but think about the story her grandmother had told last night, about the justice the town exacted all those years ago. Her aunt Freya had warned her not to trust people in Meadowmere, and Calista thought she was probably right.

Calista turned on Marble Lane, heading toward her house. She slipped her backpack off her shoulders, which had started to ache, and let it dangle from her fingers. But as she approached her house, she saw that there was a woman sitting on the top step of the front porch.

Calista was startled by the stranger, and her mind quickly raced through the possibilities of who she could be. Then she smelled lilacs—the same scent she'd detected yesterday when her premonition told her she'd have visitors.

The woman was staring down at her phone, oblivious to Calista's approach. Calista was glad for that, because it meant she had time to study her. The woman had curly red hair and was wearing a dark blazer, a pencil skirt, and tan heels. She looked professional, pragmatic. A person who came to the Wynns looking for help was usually more fidgety, uncomfortable, and nervous. This woman seemed . . . distracted.

Just then, the woman looked up and noticed Calista. She offered a small, polite smile.

"Can I help you?" Calista asked, glancing at her house. She found her father standing at the window, peering out at them. He nodded a hello to his daughter.

"I . . ." The woman stared at Calista, seeming unsure of where to start. Then she shook her head and got to her feet, holding the railing for support on her wobbly heels. On further inspection, Calista thought the woman was out of place in her outfit. Almost like it wasn't hers at all. A last-ditch effort to look pulled together, maybe.

"This was a mistake," the woman said in a rush, heading for the sidewalk. "I have to go."

Before she could flee, the woman's heel slipped in between the concrete blocks of pavement, and she flailed her arms to catch her balance. Calista quickly dropped her backpack and rushed toward the woman, taking her hand to steady her. But the moment she did, Calista's head was filled with a heavy wave of thoughts.

He's only been missing a few days.

She's just a kid, she can't help me.

Oh, Thomas. Come home. Please just—

"Thomas?" Calista asked, shocked. The woman yanked her hand away, and Calista staggered backward, nearly tripping over her backpack on the sidewalk.

Along with the woman's thoughts, Calista had seen images. She'd seen Thomas, alive and in his bedroom, listening to music as his mother came in to tell him it was time for dinner. Thomas as a baby, crawling along the tan rug in the living room. His mother, distraught and crying as she reported his disappearance to the police.

"You know my son?" the woman asked, her eyes wide and glazing over with tears. "You know him? Have you seen him?" she demanded. "I heard about the young one today, the new boy missing. Do you know where they all are?"

But Calista felt her insides sink. She didn't know where Thomas's spirit was anymore. The Tall Lady had done something to turn him into ash and he was no longer in this realm. But Thomas's mother wasn't talking about his spirit. She wanted to know where he was. Physically. Where his . . . his body was. Calista didn't know the answer to that either.

"I don't know where any of them are," Calista said, feeling her own eyes well up with tears. "I'm sorry, but I don't know."

The woman seemed incredulous. "But you know my Thomas," she said. "I can tell." The woman wiped under her nose and fixed her hair and the hem of her skirt. She tried to pull herself together.

81

It was a nervous reaction that Calista had seen before. The way people wanted to make things normal around her, normal when they realized she knew too much to be normal. It was part of their denial and acceptance, at least, that was how Mac always explained it to Calista.

Calista looked toward the house and saw that her grandmother had joined her father at the window. Her expression was troubled. In fact, Calista thought her grandmother hadn't been the same since they'd seen Edwina in her room. Then again, who would be? The spirit was terrifying.

"Would you like to come in?" Calista asked Thomas's mother. "We can talk inside."

Calista cast a nervous glance around the neighborhood, expecting at least one of her neighbors to be watching the latest client. Offer a knowing smile and wave. Her neighbors weren't like the rest of the town. The families that lived on Marble Lane had always been kind to the Wynn family, bonded by their shared situation. They lived in the oldest part of Meadowmere, the part that was still sinking. They'd been cast aside by the society they could see across the water on a clear day.

To the neighbors, the Wynns were just making their way. So when a new person stopped by the house, a friendly face would show up that night with a plate of cookies to catch up on any gossip that might slip out of Calista's mother while they sat at the kitchen table together. But that was when strangers came for charms. Not when children were missing.

"Yes," the woman said to Calista. "Yes, I think I should come inside."

Calista nodded before picking up her backpack and leading the woman up the stairs, telling her to watch her step, which made her laugh softly. The woman radiated grief, an extreme sadness that Calista could feel in her gut, enough so that she probably wouldn't be able to eat dinner later.

Sometimes Calista absorbed too much pain, pain that didn't just disappear after the client left. But she took that pain from others, lessening their burden.

The house was quiet as they got inside. Both Mac and Grandma Josie were out of sight, as they always were when Calista had to talk to a potential client.

Strangers often found it unsettling when Calista accidentally spoke out loud to the empty air across the room. They expected her to talk to *their* ghosts, not her own.

"Would you like something to drink?" Calista asked as she led the woman to the sitting room. A floorboard creaked overhead, and the woman noticeably jumped. "It's just an old house," Calista explained.

The woman smiled but didn't look any more at ease. "I'm okay," the woman said, waving off the drink suggestion.

They were quiet for a minute until Calista cleared her throat. "So how can I help you, Miss . . ." She waited for the woman to offer her name.

"Call me Sharon," she said. "Are you what they say you are?" she asked, not unkindly. "Can you really help people?"

"Sometimes," Calista said honestly.

"And you know about the missing boys, including my Thomas?"

"Only what I've heard on the news," Calista said, disliking that she had to lie. Of course she knew more than just that. But if she told Sharon about seeing Thomas's spirit, then she'd have to tell her what had happened to him. Calista was still trying to figure that part out. "I know about the . . . the three boys missing," Calista said. She wondered then if there'd been any updates on Wyland's little brother. He'd vanished, just like the others.

"Yes, three missing," Sharon repeated, pulling her brows together. And yet, hearing it confirmed, Calista still thought of the number four. Four missing kids. She was sure of it.

"These disappearances are related," Sharon said. "But the investigators won't listen to me."

"Why not?" Calista asked. Even if she hadn't known about Edwina, it seemed perfectly logical to suspect the disappearances were somehow connected. Three boys missing in the same small town within a week of each other? More than a coincidence.

"Because no one cares about us," Sharon said so simply that it was a confession. "They don't care about us out in the Flats."

She motioned toward the window. The Flats was a neighborhood on the other side of the train tracks made up of small, modest houses that were half-sunken into the mud.

It had all but been abandoned, except by those without the means to leave.

Calista studied the woman again. Although at first glance her outfit was professional, on closer inspection Calista saw that her shoes were scuffed and peeling up at the toe. Her pantyhose had runs at the knee, and her skirt was fraying at the ends. Sharon and her family lived in the forgotten section of Meadowmere, a place few ever even ventured anymore.

"I homeschool my boys," Sharon added. "I wasn't sure how long we could stay after their father left, but things were getting better. I've been working, and . . ." She trailed off and shook her head. "Not that it mattered," she added bitterly. "When Thomas disappeared, I went to the police. They asked if he had run away, run away to be with his father. But the answer is no. Thomas would never leave me and his brothers like that—leave without telling us. He's good." Tears dripped onto her cheeks and Calista's body swayed with pain. "He's a good boy."

Calista sympathized with Sharon—absorbed her pain. She wanted . . . no, she needed to help. She couldn't let this happen to another family.

"What have you heard about the other missing boy?" Calista asked. "The one before Thomas? Did your son know him?"

"No," Sharon said. "Thomas stayed in the neighborhood. He was shy, quiet." She looked down, picking at a bit of lint on her skirt. "But in a small town, kids going missing within a few days of each other, unrelated? Now tell me, how does that make any sense?"

"It doesn't," Calista agreed. She had hoped that by talking with Sharon, she'd be able to get more information in order to summon Devon Winters tonight, and perhaps find a detail the police had let slip or a connection between all the missing boys. Why had they been selected? Who would be next?

All the missing kids lived on opposite sides of town: Devon in the north, Thomas to the east, and Parker would be west. The only southern part of Meadowmere was Calista's neighborhood, and as far as she knew, no one had gone missing from there.

It would only be a matter of time before Edwina struck again. But what exactly was her endgame? What type of revenge was she planning? Until Calista knew for sure, she had no idea how to prevent it.

First, she had to figure out where the boys were being hidden—there was still a chance the others were okay. And she hoped she could find Parker Davis before it was too late for him.

Calista continued to listen as Sharon told her about Thomas's last moments at home. As a mother, Sharon questioned her own moves, her every interaction. She was stricken with guilt although she had done nothing wrong. Calista knew about Edwina coming to his window. She hated that she couldn't alleviate Sharon's guilt by telling her.

Calista thought about the Tall Lady in the classroom, hovering over Wyland. The way he had shivered when she was close to him. She then wondered how long Edwina stalked her victims. Molly had been speaking to the spirit. Was she next? Was Wyland?

"Had Thomas complained of being cold?" Calista asked suddenly.

"What?" Sharon said, wiping tears off her chin where they had collected.

"Did you notice him bundled up, or had he mentioned that he was cold leading up to his disappearance?" she asked. "And for how long?"

There was a strange flicker in Sharon's eyes, and she glanced around the room suddenly. Calista felt the shift in her demeanor.

"He'd been cold for a few days," the woman replied. "I thought he might be getting sick." Sharon swallowed hard. "But Thomas didn't complain. He never complained. The house was cold, so I kept the fire going in the wood-stove a little longer. My other sons would be sweating, but Thomas . . . he still shivered in the corner. But then—" Her lips paused midsentence, her eyes squinted. "Never mind," she said, looking away.

"Tell me," Calista said, leaning forward in her chair.

"The night he disappeared," Sharon said reluctantly. "The house was so warm. I went into his room to say

87

goodnight and discovered he was gone. And the air in the room was freezing—there was frost on the *inside* of his window. But more than that, I-I was sure that I wasn't alone. Almost like I could feel icy breath on the back of my neck. I cried out, thinking Thomas was playing a joke on me. But when I turned, there was no one else in that room. I was completely alone."

Sharon covered her face and began to cry, her shoulders shaking as she did. It was a combination of grief and fear. It was confronting the truth. After all, it was a lot easier to dismiss the supernatural when you weren't sitting in the house of a child medium.

"I'm sorry," Calista said. "I'm sorry that he's gone. I . . . I want to help. I'll look into it, okay? I'll help you find him."

Sharon looked up then, and Calista could swear that the mother knew. She knew her son was no longer alive. She knew this was a recovery. But for her part, Sharon sucked back her tears and straightened her posture. Calista could feel her bravery, that she'd been a fiercely protective mother. That she would do anything for her children. It made the pain that much worse.

Sharon unclicked the lock on her purse and fished out a receipt from a drugstore. She quickly jotted down a number on the back and held it out to Calista.

"Please," she said. "If you find him . . . call me."

Calista promised that she would and stood when Sharon got up. She walked her to the door in silence, and the woman whispered a short goodbye before exiting the house. The moment she was gone, Calista turned around and was startled by her grandmother standing in the foyer.

"You should have told that woman that her boy was dead," Grandma Josie said very sternly. "Never give them false hope, Callie. I've taught you better than that."

Calista's shoulders slumped.

"I couldn't," she said. "I couldn't tell her that he was dead. Not to mention that I saw a ghost lady kill his ghost. Or his spirit. Or whatever she did!" She could feel herself breathing heavily, sucking in air like there wasn't enough in the room. Her heart pounded in her ears. "I don't even know how it happened! I don't understand the rules, Gran! Thomas . . . He's gone, and I don't know why!"

That was the thought that pained Calista the most. Thomas had come to her for help. Instead, something awful had happened to him in her room. Maybe she should have never summoned him at all. But second-guessing wouldn't bring him back and it wouldn't set him free.

"Sharon wouldn't have believed me even if I did tell her what happened to Thomas," Calista added solemnly. "It would have hurt her."

Grandma Josie seemed to think it over before adjusting her shawl. "Trust me, Callie," she said. "Secrets never save anybody." And then she shuffled quietly toward the kitchen.

10

THERE WAS SOMETHING bothering Calista about Parker Davis being missing. She considered it as she grabbed her grandmother's books and spread them out once again on the living room rug. Parker wasn't thirteen, not like the other two boys or her aunt Virginia. So why would Edwina want him?

Unless . . . Unless she was using him to lure his thirteen-year-old brother, Wyland. Then again, why not just take Wyland? And Molly, she was only six and Edwina had been talking with her. So what exactly was the Tall Lady playing at? It didn't make any sense.

Calista hoped the volumes of Wynn history could help her. They went all the way back to Grandma Josie's great-grandmother. But they were mostly simple charms and summoning spells, things a medium could use to make a living. There had been no knowledge of any curse back then. The Wynns had been doing very well in Meadowmere, operating a successful family business in the time when mysticism thrived.

A thought occurred to Calista. Could this be a new curse that Edwina was trying to enact at her family's expense? A curse on the entire town? She returned to the volume that talked about lost souls. But there was nothing even close to fitting the situation with Thomas or any of the other boys.

Frustrated, Calista closed the book. Her best tool now was her own intuition and investigation skills.

There was a jingling of keys in the lock of the front door. When her mother opened it, announcing her arrival home, Molly came running inside like a windstorm as she called Calista's name.

She was too little to truly understand what had happened with the missing boy, but she was a medium. She sensed the panic more than others.

Molly found Calista in the living room, poring over Grandma Josie's old books.

"Callie," Molly said, out of breath. Her bottom lip jutted out. "A boy is *missing*! The whole town is looking for him."

"I know," Calista replied, glancing at her mother, who was texting someone on her phone. "It's very sad. I hope they find him soon."

Molly came close to her sister and put her small hands on either side of Calista's cheeks, her fingers freezing cold. "Is he with the Tall Lady?" Molly whispered, wide-eyed. There was a flash of fear there. "Did she . . . Did she hurt him?"

The question made Calista's insides turn with dread. She quickly pulled her little sister into a gentle hug. "I don't know," Calista said honestly, quiet enough for her mother not to hear their conversation. "But you're safe here, okay?" she added. "There's a protection spell on the house. You just make sure you tell me if you see that spirit again, all right?"

Molly nodded. "Okay," she said as she straightened up. She patted Calista's head like she was doing a good job, a parent figure at six years old.

In the doorway to the living room, their mother looked over with a stricken expression. Unaware of Molly's questions, Nora glanced around at the books on the floor before there was a pause of realization. Her jaw tightened when she looked at Calista again.

"Molly," Nora said, but kept her gaze on her older daughter, "go into the kitchen and fix yourself a snack. I need to talk to Callie for a moment."

"Can I have cookies?" Molly asked, turning back to look at her. "Please!"

"Sure," Nora said, waving her forward. Molly yelped gleefully and ran from the room.

Calista watched after her sister, her heart swelling with love. To be honest, she was glad Molly was home where she could keep an eye on her.

Mac appeared in the hallway then, tilting his head as he listened in to whatever Calista's mother was about to say.

As she stepped through the doorway, Nora looked down

at the books on the floor again, and then around at the room. "Your father here?" she asked, her voice stern.

Calista nodded, worried about her mother's impending lecture.

"Mac, what have you let her get into?" Nora demanded. "We'd talked about this. You promised you'd never let her get involved in anything dangerous."

In the doorway, Mac winced, looking regretful. Nora turned back to Calista.

"You're not allowed to keep secrets from me," Nora told her. "I know I may not have gifts like you do, but I have some common sense. And I know not to let my twelve-year-old walk headfirst into a dangerous situation."

"Mom," Calista said, guilt-stricken and a bit embarrassed to be in trouble, "I'm sorry. But I didn't mean to—"

"What?" Nora asked, hand on her hip. "Keep it from me? Then what were you doing last night? I bet you were trying to contact those missing kids, weren't you?"

"One of them," Calista said. "And I would have told you, but—"

"But you didn't think I'd understand," her mother said for her. "You don't have to be psychic to know when something is a bad idea, Callie. And this is downright dangerous. Not only are those kids missing, and I'm assuming . . . dead,"—she flinched at the word—"but now that you're involved, people are going to start talking. We don't want that. Your dad and I decided long ago that we would try to give you and your sister a mostly normal life. Some charms here and there, sure. But not this. Not something that can get you hurt."

"He came to me," Calista said softly. "One of the missing boys. He was in my room yesterday morning. And when I figured out who he was, I thought I could help him."

Although her mother was sympathetic to the boy's plight, she was also protective of Calista. "I'm guessing it didn't go well," Nora said, her expression strained. "What happened to him?"

Calista opened her mouth to answer, to tell her mother all about the Tall Lady and the family history, but at that moment, there was a brush of cold air over her legs. It startled her silent.

In the doorway, Mac looked around, sensing it too. Something was . . . off. Something was *here*. Calista didn't have time to explain the entire situation with Thomas to her mother. Not right now.

"The spirit moved on," Calista told her quickly, getting to her feet. "He couldn't remember what happened to him, but I helped him move on."

Her mother's face softened with grief. "I'm sorry to hear that he died," she said. "He was young. Too young. Was it an accident?" her mother asked.

Calista shrugged, doing her best to keep her focus on her mother. What she really wanted to do was run around the house and search for the presence that was hanging around.

The house was protected, so it might be a kind spirit. Maybe one of the missing boys.

"He didn't get a chance to say before he moved on," Calista told her mother, continuing to lie. "But . . . with everything that happened, I took your advice."

Her mother smiled suspiciously. "Well, that would be a first. Advice about what?"

"I called Aunt Freya," Calista said. "She's coming to visit tomorrow."

"Tomorrow?" Nora asked, her voice high-pitched. "Well, I wish you would have told me sooner." Calista's mother immediately began sweeping her eyes around the house, ticking off things she wanted to do. "I need to make up the guest room," she said. "And I have to get to the grocery store." She paused and looked at Calista. "Should I make a pie? I should make a pie," she answered herself.

"It's okay, Mom," Calista said. "I promise she'll be fine without a pie."

Nora laughed at herself, brushing back her hair. "Yes, I suppose you're right," she said, and turned to the window, as if waiting for Freya already. "Oh, how I've missed our Freya," she added quietly.

Calista's mother and aunt were very close. In fact, it was how Nora had met Mac in the first place. Nora had grown up in a different part of Meadowmere, closer to the city. She'd been friends with Freya in high school, but not the type that hung out every day. They were in-school friends. But one afternoon, as her mother tells it, Freya got a funny look on her face. She told Nora that she just *had* to come by the house after school.

So Nora Robetelli came to the Wynn family home. And almost like he sensed her coming—which he swears he didn't—Mac Wynn was out on the front lawn planting Grandma Josie's annuals a week early. According to legend, time stopped that day. Mac picked the prettiest of the flowers and handed it to Nora as she walked past him into his house. They smiled at each other.

By the end of that day, she was his girlfriend. And Freya claimed she'd seen it all happen before it did. Which was why she'd invited Nora over in the first place.

True or not, Calista's parents were together from then on—high school sweethearts. And her mother gave the credit to her best friend, Freya.

But through the years, Freya traveled all over the world— never married, and no kids. She and Nora didn't talk quite so often. After Mac died, Freya was around to help, but the same love that bound people together could sometimes be a barrier when it turned to grief. Calista wasn't sure they had spoken much since her father's funeral.

Looking at her mother now, Calista saw only loving anticipation for her friend's return. Just behind that was a layer of loneliness. It hit Calista a bit hard, that emotion coming from her mother. It reminded her that she left her mother out of many things in her life, things she didn't think she'd understand. And of course, Nora missed her husband. She missed him every day.

"Well, I'm going to make that pie," Nora said. "Rhubarb, her favorite. But from now on," she added, pointing at Calista, "you talk to me before you get involved in anything else. Understood?"

"Understood," Calista repeated.

"Wonderful." Nora nodded. "Now, when you see your grandmother, ask her where she hid that old recipe book. I know just the pie to make."

"It's under the hutch, second cabinet to the right," Mac said, his eyes shining with emotions. Calista guessed he could feel her mother's loneliness too.

"Dad said it's in the lower cabinet of the hutch," Calista told her mother. "To the right."

Nora paused, and then nodded. "Thank you, Mac," she murmured.

There was another surge of grief before Nora smiled at her daughter and left the room. Her entrance into the kitchen was marked by Molly's happy shout.

"I've got chocolate chip!" the little girl yelled.

Calista stood in the living room among the books for a moment, wondering what she should do. It would be hard to talk to Molly alone right now without rousing her mother's suspicions. She'd find out more as soon as she could. A clue about Parker would definitely help Calista in her investigation.

But first things first. There was a presence in her house. She hoped it was Devon coming to find her. Or even Parker. Cold air was seeping up from the basement, she'd realized—from the séance room. When she thought that, she looked at her father and found him staring out the window. He was lost in a thought, far away from their current troubles.

It occurred to Calista for the first time that he was probably lonely too. He was with his family—where he wanted to be, he'd assured her many times. But he couldn't touch them. Couldn't really interact with them. And soon, Calista wouldn't be able to see him at all.

And it was that thought, the deep ache of losing her father, that spurred her into action. She didn't want anyone to suffer the way she had. It wasn't right to lose someone you loved. It just wasn't right.

She had to stop Edwina from whatever she was planning before she hurt anyone else. She had to protect her family and her town.

With the chill crawling over her skin, Calista grabbed the books from the floor and started for the basement stairs, ignoring her father when he called for her to wait for him.

11

THE BASEMENT WAS like an icebox as Calista made her way down the stairs. She shivered, pressing the books to her chest to insulate against the cold. Mac appeared at the bottom of the staircase and held up his hand.

"You promised your mother," he said. "She wouldn't want you—"

But Calista walked around her father's apparition and made her way into the séance room. The décor made her feel like she was coming home. Despite the obvious danger, she felt peaceful in the séance room. The walls were draped in red velvet fabric while small lamps with dangling gold tassels cast the room in a warm hue. The room felt out of time, a throwback to a different era. It helped clients believe. Helped them get out of their own heads.

Calista set the volumes of books on the shelf near the back of the room and checked the lock on the outside door, making sure it was secured. White puffs of air slipped out of her mouth with each breath. There was definitely a spirit present, no doubt about that.

But Calista couldn't get a sense of the spirit. It wasn't talking to her. She didn't even think it was looking for her. It felt old and it smelled rotten—it wasn't a little boy.

"Who's here?" she demanded, scanning the room again. "Show yourself."

Upstairs, she had hoped it was Devon coming to find her and save her the trouble of summoning him. Around her, there was a soft noise, a static buzz. Calista winced, as it hurt her ears. And then, just as suddenly as it had begun, the sound stopped like a plunge into silence. The cold air faded, and the room quickly warmed again.

Confused, Calista looked at her father, who seemed equally alarmed.

"It's gone," he said, perplexed.

"Any sense of who or what it was?" she asked him. "Can you feel anything about the missing kids?"

"I'm sorry, Callie," Mac said. "I wish I could. But you know that even if I were alive, I wouldn't have the answers. Not the same way you do."

Mac had been a great medium, and after losing his gift, he had retained an incredible sense of intuition and strong charms. But he didn't . . . *know* things. Not as strongly as Calista did.

"Well, I'm confused," Calista said. "In my head there are *four* missing kids. But everyone keeps telling me there are three. And what about Thomas's mother? She felt the police weren't doing enough to investigate his disappearance. Is that true?"

"When it's your child, there is no amount of investigation that would be enough," Mac replied. "But I think we both know that what she's looking for is something that only you can help with. Is there anything Thomas might have told you about that morning that could lead you to where his body is?" Mac asked, careful around the topic. "His mother needs the closure, Callie. I think she was right to come to you."

"But I don't know where he is," Calista said.

"Then I think your earlier instincts were right," Mac answered. "We need to find these other kids. When we do, I'm sure Thomas's body will be there with them." His voice was somber, and Calista knew with a deep dread that her father didn't think the other missing kids were alive either.

"Should I summon Devon?" Calista asked. "What will happen if he's not dead?"

Mac shook his head. "It's never a good idea to try and summon the living," he said. "You might pull them to the other side before they're ready to go. If that boy is in trouble, clinging to life, we don't want to be the reason he passes on."

Calista hadn't thought about the danger. Which was why it was definitely a good idea to wait for her aunt. But still . . . she had to do something. Her eyes widened. "Wait," she added quickly.

Calista headed up the stairs and rushed down the hallway toward her bedroom. She dug through the nightstand drawer next to her bed, pushing aside pencils and coins, random small toys from gumball machines. She found the card stuck to the bottom, as if it had been trying to hide itself. Calista peeled it off the wood and turned it over. It was the business card she'd found tucked in her doorway: Jerimiah Winters, Realtor. In scrawled red ink, he'd asked for her to contact him.

The grief she'd felt when she first touched the card had faded slightly, rubbed off as the moments passed. But it was still there. If it was too dangerous to summon Devon, maybe the situation called for some investigative work.

While her mother and Molly were in the kitchen, Calista snuck back downstairs. There was a phone there with an outside line, private and out of earshot. The family rarely used it anymore, but they kept it just in case. Her father used to make his calls there. He would talk to his clients for hours, helping them through their troubles.

Calista hated leaving her mother out of this, especially when she had specifically asked her not to. But Nora didn't see ghosts. She had no connection to the supernatural world other than her relationships with the mediums in her family. That wasn't to say Calista didn't trust her mother's advice. She just didn't think she could fully understand the problem.

What could Calista tell her anyway? That she was hunting

down a ghost killer? Oh, yes, she was sure her mother would love that.

Calista sat down on the upholstered teal-colored chair in the corner and picked up the old-fashioned phone. She stared at the number on the card and dialed carefully. Her heart was beating quickly, like she was a runner waiting for the starting gun. Finally, the phone began to ring, and Calista set the business card on her lap, steadying it with her hand as her knee bobbed with nervousness. The phone line rang at least four times before there was a soft click.

"Hello?" the male voice asked urgently. Desperately.

"Hi, um . . ." Calista started, looking down at the card again. "My name is Calista Wynn. You, uh . . . You left a card at my house and asked me to call you."

The man sucked in a startled breath and nearly choked on it. It was immediately followed by a guttural sob. "He's gone, isn't he?" the man asked. "You've seen Devon. Is he there with you now?"

"That's not why I'm calling, sir," Calista said, standing up from the chair and letting the business card drop to the cement floor of the basement.

Calista glanced around for her father to get his advice, but he was nowhere to be seen. She needed him to help coach her through this conversation. Where had he gone?

"You're a medium," the man said, sniffling hard. "Can't you speak with him? I can pay you. I'll pay anything."

"This isn't about money, Mr. Winters," Calista replied, feeling bad for him. "I'm calling because . . ."

Calista stopped short, because sitting at the circular table in the middle of the room was a skinny, curly-haired boy with a wide grin. Calista blinked in surprise, and the boy laughed, holding up his hand in a wave.

"Can you help me?" he asked. "I think . . . I think I'm stuck." And then the ghost boy's smile faltered, as if he'd forgotten why he was there.

Calista's mouth hung open as she stared at him.

"Are you still there?" Mr. Winters asked on the phone, startling Calista into looking away. She stammered before catching her train of thought.

"Uh, yes. I'm still here," Calista replied.

"Have you seen him?" the father asked, his voice hinging on hysterical. "Just tell me if my son is dead."

Calista turned back to the boy at the table, and he seemed lost, looking around the room in confusion. It was the same look that Thomas had the morning she first saw him.

"Your son Devon?" Calista asked into the phone, loud enough for the ghost to hear. His attention snapped in her direction and he perked up.

"That's my name!" he said. "Do I know you? Are you here to help me?"

Calista wasn't going to have to search for the first missing boy. He'd just decided to show up at her house. Calista swallowed hard and bent down to pick up the business card from the floor. She slid it into her back pocket.

"I'm sorry about this, Mr. Winters," she said. "But can I call you back?"

"Call me back?" He was incensed. "Is your family going to help me? Do you have any idea what we're going through over here?"

"I understand," Calista tried to explain. "I'm going to do everything I can to help. I just . . . I need some time. Now I have to go. Goodbye." She hung up before he could argue anymore.

That was rude, Calista thought, regretting that she had to cut him off. But she *was* trying to help him. Even though the situation had become much more dire.

She turned back to Devon and found him waiting politely at the table, his pale hands folded in front of him. Calista studied him for a moment, but he seemed to have forgotten she was there. He glanced around the room, curious and unbothered.

"How did you find me?" Calista asked, drawing his attention. "How did you know to come here?"

Devon paused a long moment. "The woman showed me where you live."

"What woman?" Calista asked, trying to think if there were any mediums in the city that would have recommended her. But the Wynns were the last.

"Edwina," Devon said. "She brought me here and told me to talk to you."

Calista stood very still, terrified. The Tall Lady had brought him there?

Calista looked toward the high window of the basement, scared she'd see Edwina's face pressed against the glass. Thankfully, she found only pavement and the dying grass of the front yard.

Walking carefully around the table, keeping her eyes on Devon, Calista came to pause next to him, looking him over.

"But *why* are you here?" she asked. "You must be searching for something."

The boy paused to think about that, but then he shook his head. "I'm not sure," he replied. "But can you help me with something? My feet are stuck."

He made a show of trying to lift his feet off the cement floor, but they barely moved. He was barefoot, his toenails turned black. Calista took a step away from him.

"Where are you, Devon?" she asked. "Where are you right now?"

He looked up at her and laughed. "With you, of course."

"Think, Devon," she said very calmly. "Where are *you*?"

Those words hit him differently, and Devon shifted, pulling his brows tightly together. And just then, the temperature in the room plummeted again. But this was not a breeze. It was more like Calista had suddenly been plunged into icy lake water. Her scared breath came out in a foggy puff.

Calista spun around, checking for the Tall Lady, sure that she was there. She hugged herself for warmth, and when she didn't see Edwina, Calista turned back to Devon. He seemed so thin, frail. She didn't want the same thing to happen to him that had happened to Thomas.

"You have to go," Calista said sternly. "Leave, Devon. Hide."

His lips parted, and for a moment his eyes widened in terror, widened so large and grotesquely that Calista cried out and fell back another step. And then, Devon faded out into nothing. Disappearing before he could be turned to ash.

Calista stood an extra moment as she shivered, stunned as she stared at the empty space. She checked that she was still alone in the room before rubbing her skin to get warmth on her arms. It was still so cold. She needed to talk to her father.

Suddenly, the smell of rot was all around her, moldy and oozing. There was still a spirit in the house, but it wasn't Devon or even Edwina. The smell . . . it was evil. Possibly demonic.

Calista knew she had to do something. She wouldn't let it hurt anyone she loved.

She ran for the stairs, taking them two at a time.

"Molly!" she called.

Where was her sister?

12

WHEN CALISTA GOT into the main hallway of her house, she was alarmed to find the temperature hadn't risen. The smell of rot hung heavy in the air, like something molded over and seeping. Her feet left imprints in the frosted wood of the floor as she started for the kitchen, where Mac was standing in the doorway, staring into the room.

"Where were you?" Calista whispered to her father, stopping next to him. "I called Mr. Winters, and then—"

But Mac wasn't listening to her. He was staring into the kitchen, his face alight with terror.

"What is it?" Calista asked, following his line of sight.

And when her eyes found her mother and sister standing together at the stove, she knew immediately that something was wrong. Her entire gut reacted to the oddness in the air.

"That is not your sister," Mac said in a low voice.

Molly let out a sharp giggle from where she stood next

to Nora at the stove, her back toward Calista and Mac. She was tilted, her weight falling differently. And the laugh didn't sound like hers. It was too piercing. The sound made Calista feel sick inside. Mac took a step into the kitchen, and the little girl's body stiffened, her hands lowering to her sides in balled-up fists.

"That's. Not. Molly," Mac said louder, and stepped further into the kitchen.

Then what is it? Calista thought.

Before Mac got even a step further into the kitchen, not-Molly looked over her shoulder to glare directly at him. Calista gasped, alarmed by both the anger in the little girl's expression and the fact that she was staring right at Mac . . . who was a ghost. No, not her little sister. Mac was right— that wasn't Molly.

Not-Molly bared her teeth at them, and Calista was struck with a sense of illness so strong, she thought she would vomit. Anger was oozing and sliding through her system as she looked at what used to be her sister.

The skin moved differently on Molly's face, taut in some areas, sagging low under her eyes. She was hollowed out, stretched thin. She didn't . . . She didn't look alive.

Calista moved into the kitchen. When she did, the creature in Molly's body sneered before clicking its tongue twice in warning. Its black eyes burned with hatred as it glared at her.

Nora turned around, humming out her surprise to see Calista in the room. "Oh, hey, honey," she said. "Where were you? I was calling for you."

Calista didn't answer, still trying to catch her breath. She kept walking, but when she got closer to her sister and mother at the stove, not-Molly growled, low in her throat.

Suddenly, the creature spun and shoved Nora directly toward the stove, where spaghetti sauce was simmering, water boiling. Calista yelled for her mother, panic making her jump forward as if she could catch her.

Nora lost her balance, but as she fell forward into the stove, she quickly put out her arms to catch herself. There was a sizzle as her hand touched the blue flames of the burner. Calista's mother cried out in pain.

"Mom, are you okay?" Calista shouted, taking her by the shoulders to ease her back from the stove.

Next to them, not-Molly watched menacingly. Calista swallowed hard, keeping her distance from the creature as she tended to her mother.

Nora stood a moment, still shocked. The side of her hand pulsed red and she winced as she looked it over. Calista quickly grabbed a clean dish towel, wet it with cold water from the sink, and then drizzled it with honey before handing it to her mother.

Still grimacing, Nora gently wrapped the towel around her injured hand. Then, she looked down at her younger daughter.

"Why did you do that, Molly?" she asked, anger clinging to the edges of her voice. "You *hurt* me. You can't play games around the stove. You know better."

Calista stood silent, terrified as she stared down into the beady eyes of not-Molly. Would it try to hurt their mother again? But then color suddenly returned to Molly's face.

The little girl blinked quickly, her lips pouting as she let out a whimper. "I'm sorry, Mommy," she said in a tiny voice, rubbing at her eyes with the backs of her hands.

Molly started to cry, a pathetic, wounded cry that startled Nora. But Calista was relieved when her sister's sad little face glanced in her direction again. It was Molly, the real Molly—she was back.

"Aw, Molly," Nora said, squatting down to gather her in a hug. Her hand was still wrapped in the towel. "I didn't mean to get upset," her mother told her, "but you have to be more careful. That was dangerous."

"I didn't mean to," Molly sobbed. She sounded scared, but Calista wasn't sure if her sister even knew what had just happened. As Nora held her, Molly wiped at her cheeks. "My tummy hurts," the little girl murmured over her tears.

Calista wanted to reach for her little sister, comfort her. Molly had just gone through something awful, something even she had never dealt with. Poor girl. Just as Calista stepped toward her, Nora looked up, her arm protectively wrapped around Molly.

"Can you finish dinner for me?" Nora asked, sounding

worried. "I'm going to have a talk with Molly. See if I can calm her down. You'll keep an eye on the pie, too? It's in the oven."

Calista agreed with a nod, still shocked by what she'd witnessed.

The temperature in the house was quickly rising, the smell of rotting earth replaced with the scents of dinner. She was still staring at the spot where her sister had been standing as her mother left the room with Molly crying in her arms.

Wait, Calista thought. *Is Mom really safe with her? Is Molly going to be all right?*

Suddenly, Calista moved to follow after them, but Mac put up his hand to stop her. She raised her eyebrows in question, needing to know they were safe.

"Your mother's okay," Mac confirmed. "Same with Molly—for now. But we need to talk."

"What in the world just happened?" she asked her father in a hushed voice. "If that wasn't Molly—who was it?"

"It was a demon," Mac told her, his voice deadly serious. "A demon crept in and possessed your little sister's body."

Calista covered her mouth, smothering a terrified shout. She'd never seen anyone possessed before, and after what she'd just witnessed, she never wanted to again. It took Calista a moment to pull herself together, darting her eyes around the room as if the demon were still with them.

"How?" she said finally, turning to her father. "I put a protection spell on the house—I thought it was working."

Mac was clearly distraught when he met Calista's eyes. "Technically, you only blocked Edwina. Perhaps that's why she sent a demon in her place. We'll need a stronger spell. And we'll need to exorcise the demon out of your sister tonight to get rid of it permanently," he said. "It won't leave Molly unless it's forced out."

"And then what?" Calista said. "How do I protect us?"

Mac winced. "This isn't all on you, Callie," he said. "Your grandmother and I will get working on those new spells, and when your aunt gets here, I know she'll have a trick or two." He looked back over Calista's shoulder and motioned to the oven. "You'd better get that before it burns," he said.

Calista turned to see the rhubarb pie in the lighted oven was starting to bubble over the side of its tin. She did as she was asked, even though her hands shook while she slid on the oven mitts.

When she turned again, her father had disappeared, leaving her to tend a pie while her possessed sister cried in her room with their injured mother. A medium's greatest fear was possession, and it was happening to her little sister, who didn't even have her full powers yet.

Anger flooded Calista's bloodstream as she yanked open the oven door and turned the pie to make sure it cooked evenly. Red liquid spilled over the edge, hissing as it hit the hot interior of the oven.

Calista was going to banish that demon. In fact, she was so mad, she was ready to rip that demon right out of her sister's body with her bare hands. But she knew it wasn't that easy. In fact, this was a terrible time to try. Calista was far too emotional, and an attempt in this state could cause more harm than good.

So Calista waited impatiently until the pie was done and then took it out of the oven to cool. With so much nervous energy pulsing around her, she worked on dinner too. She wished her father would hurry up. Every noise made her jump. Her charm had failed to protect her family. She felt exposed.

She had to calm her thoughts. Focus her mind. She took out the lettuce and started on the salad. With her body physically distracted, her mind was able to think clearly. There had been another ghost downstairs—Devon Winters. And he'd told Calista that the Tall Lady had sent him to her house? Why? Maybe it had been a distraction. A way to keep her busy while the demon got to her sister.

Devon's ghost may have been a distraction, but he had offered her a clue. His feet were stuck, he'd said. That could mean a number of things, but not when Calista considered what she knew about Edwina's past. The first children that she took all those years ago were killed at the marshes. If Devon had sunk, been sucked into the ground just like Edwina's old shack, that might explain his inability to move. His body could be there right now, near the ruin of Edwina's place. It would be hard to find him in all that mud, but at least they'd be looking. At least they'd be doing *something*.

Maybe Calista would be able to talk to him again to get more detail on where he was. But first, she had to deal with the demon currently possessing her little sister.

"Thank you, Callie," Nora said, startling Calista as she swept back into the kitchen. "You're a lifesaver."

"No problem," Calista replied. As Calista used the wooden spoon to stir the spaghetti sauce, Nora came to peek over her daughter's shoulder. "How's your hand?" Calista asked her, turning around. Her burn was now wrapped in a gauze bandage.

"It'll be fine," Nora said, waving away the concern. But Calista could tell by the way she held her hand in front of her that it still hurt. "No idea what got into your sister," Nora added, glancing back toward the hall. Her brow pulled together. "Molly's never done anything like that before."

"How's . . . How's Molly feeling?" Calista asked.

"Better, I think," her mother said, tasting the sauce before grabbing some salt and shaking it in. "She had a stomachache. Maybe that's why she acted out. I don't know. Actually," she added, turning to Calista, "would you mind getting her ready for dinner? She needs to wash up. I'll put the pasta in the water."

"Sure," Calista said, although nervous jitters twisted in her stomach. She had to admit that she was a little afraid of what she'd find in her sister's room. But her nerves had calmed enough for her to gather her courage.

She stared down the hall toward the bedrooms, her palms

clammy with anticipation.

"Grandma Josie," she whispered into the air, wondering where her grandmother had been all afternoon. When there was no response, she glanced around. "Dad?" she asked.

Mac appeared immediately, although he looked worried. "Grandma Josie is working on a special exorcism chant," he said. "But I need you to go in there to make sure that demon doesn't hurt your sister in the meantime. Don't get too close, either. We don't want it jumping bodies."

"*What?*" Calista said, alarmed. "It can do that?"

Mac winced before nodding regretfully. "It's possible. But not if you keep your guard up," he told her. "Just remember, it's all about confidence, Callie. You've got to believe harder than they do. You've got this."

And with that, her father disappeared again into the basement with Grandma Josie.

"I felt more *confident* before I knew it could jump into my body," Calista whispered after him. Frightened for herself, but also for her sister, Calista made the walk to Molly's room.

The moment she stepped up to the door, she could feel a cold breeze against her bare toes. The sensation sent a chill all the way up her legs and over her arms, swarming her face. Well, that wasn't an encouraging sign.

Calista closed her eyes, steadying herself. She had to remain calm, just like her father had told her. She gripped the door handle and pushed into the room.

She immediately winced, the smell of rotten eggs hitting

her nose. She pinched her nostrils closed just as ice-cold air swept over her, making her shiver.

And there, in the corner, was Molly. Or the thing pretending to be Molly. Because the demon had clearly been expecting her. It was still dressed in Molly's school uniform, but now her sister's body was hovering slightly off the floor in the corner of the room. Smiling so wide it split the little girl's lip. Blood trickled down her chin.

Calista refused to give away how scared she was, how worried, so instead she closed the door behind herself and locked it. The demon tilted Molly's head, watching curiously.

"Who are you?" Calista demanded. "What do you want with my sister?"

The demon slowly lowered itself until Molly's feet touched the wood floor again.

"I'm just the messenger," the demon said, its voice thick and raspy. Unnatural. The pitch of it sent chills over Calista's skin. "Edwina has the bodies you're looking for," the demon continued. "She said to come and get them."

Calista was doubtful. "That's nice of her to hand them over," she said. "So where are they?"

"The marshes, of course." Molly's mouth smiled again, another trickle of blood. Calista winced, not wanting to see her sister hurt anymore. "But you already know that," the demon added. It tilted its head, studying Calista. The eyes were pure black and filled with malice.

Calista had figured the boys were at the marshes, but

the demon gave the information so easily. Too easily. "The marshes are a big place," she told the demon. "How can I find them?"

"There's a small building," the creature said with a slithering smile. "Little more than four walls and tragedy. You'll find the children there. Come alone," the demon added.

"No," Calista said, sounding brave. "I think I'll bring help."

The demon flinched, seemingly surprised that she had dismissed its command. "You don't get to decide," the demon snapped, its eyes flashing angrily.

"I do," Calista said, although she could feel the temperature in the room dropping further, the acrid smell growing stronger. The demon inched toward her, and Calista had to force herself to stay in place. If she retreated, she would look weak. And then she'd have no control over what would happen next.

"Perhaps we do this my way," the demon growled, taking three fast steps in her direction.

Calista's heart jumped into her throat, and without meaning to, she moved back until she bumped into the closed door. Her heart fluttered a terrified pulse.

There was a sudden shift of air. Calista looked to her side as her grandmother appeared next to her. Grandma Josie stared down the demon, and it retracted from her steely gaze.

"You give me back my granddaughter!" Grandma Josie

yelled at the creature, her expression fierce. She made several movements with her swollen fingers, murmuring a Latin phrase. Calista knew immediately what her grandmother needed her to do.

Mimicking the words and movements, Calista took a step toward the demon, putting force behind each syllable. "Exi ergo," Calista said in Latin. "Vade retro, daemonium." She shifted her fingers to form symbols. Wind began to spin in the room, papers fluttering beneath their tacks pressed into the wall, the curtains billowing. "Depart," Calista said in English, shoving her palms toward the creature. "Go back, demon."

The demon groaned, writhing. It let out an unearthly screech, worse than nails on a chalkboard. Its hair flapped around its face, its eyes squeezed shut.

With her grandmother at her side, Calista forced the demon backward, repeating the words just after her grandmother would speak them. The storm in the room grew stronger—and small objects began to swing and swirl in a circle above them. Molly's toys danced in the air, the sheets stripping from her bed.

The demon scuttered back until it bumped into the wall next to Molly's closet, its arms covering its face as it began to howl in pain.

"Redire ad inferos," Calista murmured, and then did one last movement with her fingers.

The moment she pulled her fingers free from the knots

she had created, the shifting air in the room stopped. For a moment, all the items from Molly's room hung suspended, as if in the eye of a hurricane. Then they dropped at once to the floor in a loud clatter.

Molly's body began to shudder, twisting left and right, her arms banging against the wall as the demon shook her entire being. Calista moved forward to hold her little sister so she wouldn't get hurt, but then suddenly, the demon looked up toward the ceiling and opened its mouth wide. Black smoke poured out.

"Open the window, quickly," Grandma Josie said, pointing a shaking finger in that direction.

Calista dashed over to the window and quickly yanked it open. Instinctively, she put her palm over her mouth, afraid the demon would come for her instead. The wind in the room picked up again, and Calista jumped to the side as the current drove the smoke out of the house. When the last bit of the demon poured out the window, Calista slammed it shut.

There was a whimper, and then Molly collapsed to the floor. Calista raced over to gather her up, holding her little sister close as she woke, crying softly. Her body was cold, limp. She had cuts on her lip, bruises on her arms. Calista carried her sister over to the bed and sat her on the mattress before grabbing a blanket to wrap over her shoulders.

Grandma Josie came to sit next to her protectively. "We've got you, Jellybean," Grandma Josie told Molly, even though the little girl couldn't hear her. But Calista was sure that her sister felt the love, because she stopped crying.

Calista rubbed her sister's shoulder, but Molly continued to shake. Her skin was pale and circles had darkened under her eyes.

"Are you okay?" Calista asked softly.

Molly shook her head no, her bottom lip sticking out. She was just about to cry again. It broke Calista's heart to see her go through this.

"I'm here," Calista told her. "I banished the demon. It won't come back. I'm going to protect you, okay?"

Molly hitched in a breath, lifting her brown eyes to meet Calista's. "Y-You said that before," she murmured, and then cried softly.

Calista quickly gathered her into a hug, but the truth was, she *had* promised Molly she'd protect her, and she had failed. She felt a pit in her stomach. How could she have let this happen?

Mac appeared in the room and immediately rushed toward Molly. "Is she okay?" he asked. "Did it hurt her?" He reached out to touch her hair, but his hand glided right through the brown curls.

"It could have been worse," Calista said quietly. "At least physically." She pulled back from Molly and adjusted the blanket on her shoulder. "I'm going to talk to Daddy for a moment, okay?"

Molly nodded and wiped haphazardly at the tears on her

cheeks. "Okay," she responded in a sad little voice.

Grandma Josie stayed next to Molly while Calista walked toward the window, her father close behind her. When he got next to her, she kept her voice low.

"That was terrifying," she told him. "Where were you?"

"I found a spell that should be able to keep out demons," he said. "But . . . did the creature say anything? Did it say what it wanted?"

"It had a message from Edwina," Calista whispered.

"I knew that witch had sent it," Mac replied, placing his palm over his mouth as he waited to hear the rest of the story.

After a check on Molly, who sat quietly as she sniffled on her bed, Calista began to pace the room. She looked over at her father. "The demon said the missing kids are in a building at the marshes," Calista told her father quietly. "Do you think that's true? What's even out there?"

"Nothing," Mac said with a shrug. "But we have no way of knowing for sure without going out there. Problem is, your grandmother and I can't go with you. Not without . . . Not without losing some of ourselves."

Mac and Grandma Josie hadn't left the property since they returned from the grave. There was no telling what would happen if they did—they might lose their tether to their lives, forget everything. Their spirits could be left to roam the earth, not knowing why they couldn't pass on. It was too big a risk.

"So what do I do?" Calista asked. "Should I call the sheriff?"

"And tell him what?" Mac asked, shaking his head. "Molly got possessed and the demon that did it told you where the missing kids are? That won't go over well." He folded his hands on top of his head, watching the ceiling as he thought it over. "My sister is going to be here tomorrow," he said. "We'll let your aunt Freya handle that part. She knows the sheriff personally. She'll explain."

Behind Mac, Grandma Josie nodded. "Wait for Freya," she agreed. "No one in this family is going out to those marshes. Not a single one of you."

13

CALISTA WAS FRUSTRATED as she sat in her room. She had completed the new protection spell her father made up, one that banned demons, but she still didn't feel entirely safe. How could she, after the past few days? And now she was helpless—just waiting around while children were missing, her sister had been possessed, and a curse to take Calista's powers was still looming.

Calista considered breaking her promise by summoning Devon to see if he could tell her more about where he was. Maybe then she could find Parker before it was too late. But what if she let in another vengeful spirit instead? She couldn't take the chance after what had happened to Molly. The little girl hadn't spoken a word at dinner. She had barely even eaten.

For now, Molly was sleeping in their mother's room. Calista had told Nora that Molly had fallen out of bed, causing the obvious cuts and bruises. Their mother seemed to believe the cover story and doted on Molly accordingly.

Calista wanted to do more to protect her little sister, but she'd promised to wait for her aunt Freya. As hard as that was, she knew it was the best idea for now. She lay in her bed with her homework spread out on her sheets, even though she couldn't concentrate enough to get anything done.

Calista could hear the faint ringing of the phone downstairs in the séance room. She assumed it was Mr. Winters calling back about his son. She didn't mean to ignore him, but she didn't know how to tell him that his son was never coming home. At least if she found the boy's body, she could offer him some closure.

When the phone stopped ringing, Calista looked through her notebook at her missing assignments. She was falling behind at school, which stressed her out. But then, her mother had told her at dinner that school was cancelled for the rest of the week because of the three disappearances. The superintendent wanted to take precautions after Parker had gone missing from school.

There was a tap on Calista's window, startling her. She stared in that direction, guessing it was a bug flapping against the glass. But instead, there was another small tap. Very deliberate.

Frightened, Calista got out of bed and slowly approached her window. She checked for temperature changes, strange scents hanging in the air—but there was nothing out of the ordinary. Still, her heart was in her throat. When she reached the window, Calista brushed the curtain aside and then ducked out of the way before checking again. She was surprised to find a figure standing on her front lawn—a living figure. It took her a second before she realized it was Wyland Davis.

It was . . . unexpected. Confused, she held up her finger to indicate she'd be right down. *Why is he here?* she thought. *Did something else happen? And . . . how does he know where I live?*

With Wyland waiting, Calista stuffed her feet into a pair of sneakers and grabbed the sweater she'd been wearing earlier, yanking it on over her pajamas. She smoothed down her hair and quickly made her way downstairs.

The house was quiet as she got into the foyer. Her mother and sister were asleep, and her father and grandmother were in the séance room until morning. They didn't necessarily need sleep, they just liked the quiet. They said it kept things clearer for them. A way to recharge.

Calista slipped outside and slowly pulled the door shut behind her. Above her, there was a flash of lightning in the sky, followed by a distant rumble. The rain would be here soon.

Wyland came over to meet Calista, and before they even said hello, they both sat down on the top step of the front porch. Both of their postures sagged with a sense of defeat. Despair.

Wyland's curly hair was sticking out from under his base-ball hat. He was wearing a sports jersey with a long-sleeved T-shirt underneath. No jacket. Calista knew he was cold, but that he was trying his best not to show it. She could sense that he'd come there without thinking about it. He'd made a split-second decision amid a chaotic day.

"How . . . How are you?" Calista asked quietly, unsure of what else to say.

"Doing my best," Wyland replied. "My parents . . . My mom won't stop crying." He paused, swallowing hard. "I can't believe I came here," he said, looking sideways at Calista, "but I had to ask. Did you know this was going to happen?" He pulled his eyebrows together, distraught. "When you talked to me this morning, did you know my brother was missing?"

"No," Calista said immediately. "Of course not."

"But you can see things?" Wyland asked.

"I mean . . . not in that way. I can't tell the future. I can't . . ." Calista wasn't sure how to explain what she could do. Truth was, there were a lot of things she could *almost* do. If she had time to fully develop her gifts, she might be able to see the future. See the past. Do more. But in just a few days, the bulk of her gifts would be gone. "I can't do that," she said to finish the statement.

There was another flash of lightning across the sky, this one illuminating the clouds for a long second. Thunder fol-lowed, closer now. It made Calista shiver.

Wyland didn't say anything for the next few minutes. The two of them sat on the porch in an uncomfortable silence.

"I heard about you," Wyland said after a while. He paused and Calista could feel a spike of fear radiate off him. "I heard you can speak to the dead," he stated.

Calista didn't want to reply. Of all the things she could do, it was her best talent. But it was also the creepiest. She imagined it was the biggest reason the other kids stayed away from her.

"I can sometimes," she told him, downplaying it.

His lips pouted, as if he might cry. When he looked at her again, his dark eyes were shining with tears. "Have you seen my brother, Calista?" he asked. "Is he dead?"

"I haven't seen him," she said, touching his arm to offer comfort. When she did, a jolt of knowledge shot through her.

She saw Wyland and Parker playing basketball in the driveway, Wyland lifting his little brother up high so he'd have a better shot at the basket. She watched them on vacation, riding a Ferris wheel together. Wyland was kind to his little brother, genuinely kind. And of course, she could feel the absolute devastation he was experiencing.

But what bothered Calista the most right at that moment was the knowledge that she might have at least part of an answer. She might know where Parker was being kept. And she couldn't share it.

A jet flew overhead, the rumbling shaking the stairs as it passed. Wyland looked up at it, seeming surprised, but everyone in this part of Meadowmere had gotten so used to the sound of planes that they didn't even notice them anymore.

Calista looked back at her house. All the lights were out. It was nearly ten o'clock, and her mother was long asleep. Calista should listen to her father and grandmother, wait for her aunt, who always knew what to do, but as Wyland's pain continued to wash over her, she couldn't stop the words from slipping out.

"Something . . . ," she started, and felt him turn to her. "Something happened earlier."

"What?" he asked, seeming to sense she was about to tell him a very important detail.

"How much do you believe about me and my family?" Calista asked tentatively.

Wyland's lips parted, but he didn't answer right away. He searched her face as if debating, then he shrugged. "If I'm honest," he started, "up until today, I'd say not much. But now with my brother missing, I'm ready to believe in anything that will bring him home."

As his dark eyes held hers, Calista knew she couldn't keep it from him until tomorrow. It wasn't right. Parker was his brother.

Another lightning bolt flashed, reflected in Wyland's eyes, quickly followed by rolling thunder. An impending storm close enough to leave electricity in the air.

"I talked to a spirit tonight," Calista said. Wyland gasped, his expression stricken. "Not your brother," Calista clarified quickly. "But it . . . It was one of the other missing boys. He told me . . . Well . . ."

She paused, because it wasn't just Devon who had made her suspect the marshes—the demon had told her about them directly. Practically invited her. Red flag, for sure. But at the same time . . . Calista was certain the missing boys were there. She had no intention of sharing with Wyland *how* she had gotten that information, though. That was Wynn family business.

"They're in the marshes," Calista said quickly. "A small building. I think that's where all the missing kids are."

Wyland's eyes widened as he let out a relieved breath. Without waiting for any more details, Wyland took out his phone. Calista's stomach clenched.

"Who are you calling?" she asked, her voice louder than she intended.

"My parents," Wyland said as if it were obvious. He stood up from the stairs, stomping down to the sidewalk. "Mom!" he shouted into the phone. "We need to call the sheriff."

Calista stood and watched after him. Her family had told her to wait for her aunt. Now Calista knew she'd just started something big; uncertainty began to swirl around her. As Wyland jogged to where his bike was lying in the grass, he looked back at Calista.

"Thanks, Callie," he said, using her nickname. It startled her, and it seemed to startle him too, because he stared at her for a long moment. But then his attention was pulled back to the phone. "Yeah," he said to his mother. "I'm still here."

Calista felt the first drops of rain hit her cheeks. There was another flash of lightning, followed by thunder loud enough to make her jump.

Wyland balanced the phone between his ear and his shoulder as he got on his bike. "The marshes," he said to his mother. "Some building, I guess. I'm heading home now." He clicked on the speakerphone and Calista could hear his mother frantically shouting, screaming for her husband. Wyland held the phone against the handlebar and began pedaling as fast as he could down the street.

Calista stayed frozen in place, unsure of what to do. Unsure if she'd made the right decision. But at the same time, there was a bit of hope. They might find those missing kids tonight. Maybe, just maybe, she might have saved Parker Davis's life.

14

AS CALISTA WALKED back into her house, the rain had already begun to fall more steadily. She closed the door, but when she turned, she found her grandmother in the living room. Grandma Josie was rocking slowly in her chair, her feet tapping on the floor. Calista was immediately stricken with guilt. She could tell by the pace of Grandma Josie's foot taps that she was upset.

"I'm sorry," Calista said. "I . . . I couldn't keep it from him. It didn't seem right."

"It feels that way sometimes," Grandma Josie said, her voice scratchy with age and exhaustion. "But that's why I've always told you to keep your emotions out of it. You need to learn that there is a time and place. And right now, that boy is going to bring the entire town down to those marshes. She won't like that."

"I don't care what Edwina likes," Calista said. "I had a chance to save Parker. It couldn't wait, Gran."

Grandma Josie nodded like she understood the sentiment and kept on rocking. She didn't say anything else, and Calista took that as her cue to leave. The thunder rumbled loudly outside, rattling the windows.

As she headed to her room, Calista first stopped by her mother's room, easing the door open to peek in at Molly. Her sister looked a little gray, but otherwise, she was asleep under the covers, their mother's arm wrapped around her. Molly looked restless, though. Calista wondered how long the aftereffects of possession lasted. Tomorrow, she was going to spoil Molly. Cookies and cartoons all day.

Calista closed the door and walked back to her room. Her father hadn't spoken to her since she came inside, but like Grandma Josie, he probably knew that she had told Wyland about his brother. She wondered if he was disappointed in her, too.

After returning to her room, Calista got back into bed. In the distance, she heard police sirens. It made her stomach coil with anxiety, but she hoped they'd find Parker tonight. She even wondered if they would thank her—bring a little fame to the Wynn family. The kind people appreciate instead of disdain.

Calista picked up her phone and saw a message from her aunt Freya. She was scared to open it, afraid of what her aunt might say. She should have guessed that Freya would know what she had set into motion. She was, after all, a bit of a mind reader.

I'll be there at 6 a.m. sharp, the text read. It's already on the news.

Calista quickly clicked out of the message and opened an app to look at the local news. Sure enough, at the top of the page was a breaking report.

Tip leads investigators to the Meadowmere marshes in search of three missing boys.

Calista sat up in bed and tuned in to the live report. Olivia Ferrera was on the scene, police lights flashing behind her. She was under a tent and the sound of rain pouring down meant she had to speak louder to be heard over the noise. There were so many people, at least a hundred by the look of it. Lightning flashed in the background, and Olivia paused to let the thunder pass before speaking again. This was an even bigger story than Calista had anticipated, and her nervousness climbed higher.

Calista could see a small lookout tower in the background, searchlights trained on it. Rain was pouring down, soaking everything. It must have been impossibly muddy at the marshes, and she worried about the safety of the vehicles parked in the background. They might sink into the ground. But mostly, Calista couldn't believe how quickly everyone had gathered there. She began to bite her nails in anticipation.

There would be grief, of course, when they found the bodies of the other missing boys. But hopefully she would get to see Parker being lowered down from the tower, walking away with a blanket over his shoulders into his mother's waiting arms.

As Calista watched on her screen, a park ranger climbed the ladder up to the tower and slipped inside the building, his flashlight swooping around, shining through the windows as he searched the interior. The wait felt like eternity. And then, he poked his head out.

Calista was breathing fast, waiting for the news. But before the ranger reported anything, she could already see that his expression was filled with frustration. He looked around for the sheriff, using his palm to block some of the lights shining on him. And then the ranger gave a definitive shake of his head, saying "no."

The reporter visibly faltered before turning back to the camera. "It appears there's no sign of the missing Meadowmere boys," Olivia Ferrera said. Thunder rumbled. Olivia touched her earpiece, rain pouring down in the background of her shot. She looked cold. "A press conference is expected tomorrow," Oliva added. "For now, the Meadowmere police department wants everyone to go home and be sure to lock your doors."

Calista was stunned. The missing kids weren't there.

She shouldn't have believed the demon. Of course she shouldn't have. But she had really wanted to help. She thought she could.

And Wyland . . . He would never trust her again now. Had he told the police where he'd gotten the information?

Did this mean she'd be in trouble? She had made a mess of things. At least her aunt Freya would be there in the morning to help her explain. She would know what to do.

Calista wrapped her arms around herself and stared out her darkened window. Those boys were out there somewhere. She had to find them. She just had to. The smell of turned earth—a grave—drifted inside her nose. A knot formed in her gut: the kind you felt when you anticipated something difficult to come. Outside, the thunderstorm continued, streams of rainwater pouring down her windowpane from the gutter near the roof.

Lightning flashed, and when the thunder rumbled, Calista curled up on her side and tucked her hands under her cheek. She didn't fall asleep until the rain finally stopped a few hours later.

15

AUNT FREYA ARRIVED in a flurry of excitement and dread. Calista was sure that her aunt would be upset with her, so she woke up early to put the coffee on, set out the pie, and make sure her hair was combed and her socks matched. It might not defuse the anger entirely, but it couldn't hurt.

When the taxi pulled up, Calista was already looking out the front window. She saw her aunt lean between the seats to hand the driver some money, and then motion for him to honk to alert the family of her arrival. Which the driver did, twice. Never mind it was 5:59 a.m.

"She's here!" Calista called, and her father appeared instantly.

They hadn't said more than a simple hello when Calista passed him in the hallway this morning. He wasn't ignoring her, necessarily. Instead he seemed lost in thought, considering the options. Mac always got quiet in times like that. Grandma Josie sat patiently in her chair, a soft smile as she waited to see her eldest living daughter.

While Mac stood by the door, Calista's mother took a minute to retie Molly's hair ribbon and smooth down her dress. Calista's sister had also been quiet that morning, looking like someone recovering from the flu. She hadn't said much, even when Calista gave her a cookie at breakfast.

"Well," Nora said to Calista, motioning to the door, "go help your aunt with her bags."

"Right," Calista said, opening the door to jog outside.

Freya was standing at the back of the taxi while the driver pulled her oversize bag out of the trunk with considerable effort. The bag was huge, easily the size of Molly. Calista had no idea how long her aunt would be staying with them.

"Thank you, darlin'," Freya told the taxi driver, and handed him some folded dollar bills for a tip.

"You have a good day," the man said, smiling at her before returning to the driver's seat and pulling away from the curb.

Freya took a deep breath of chilly morning air, and then furrowed her brow disappointedly as she looked around the neighborhood. Calista stood on the sidewalk, waiting for her aunt to acknowledge her. Freya obviously knew she was there.

For her part, Freya was the prettiest woman Calista had seen. Unconventionally so, of course. She wore her long dark hair in pinned curls at the base of her neck—the same style for as long as Calista could remember. Her clothing was always vintage, dresses from the 1950s. She was currently wearing a belted brown polka-dot dress with brown heels. Her coat was open, a slim wool jacket, something very French. She wore bright pink blush on her high cheekbones and a dark red color on her full lips. Calista had never seen her without makeup. She was ageless. Even in the family albums, she looked almost exactly the same as she did now, standing at the curb of 11 Marble Lane.

"I dare say this block is two inches lower than it was the last time I was here," Freya said to no one at all. "I suppose the whole neighborhood will just keep sinking until it's gone." She turned sharply to look at Calista, her big brown eyes scanning her over. "Happy almost birthday, Callie," she said, and then motioned to her giant suitcase. "Go ahead and get that inside for me, will you? I need to hug your mother something fierce."

"Oh, okay," Calista said quickly.

Calista rushed forward to grab the handle of the suitcase as her aunt moved past her and took the steps, her heels clicking on the wood. Nora was waiting at the open front door, a smile plastered on her face.

"Freya!" she sang out as the two embraced.

Calista felt the warmth radiate off them, a tidal wave of love. It nearly took her breath away. Behind them, she could see Molly's figure standing politely at the bottom of the stairs. It hurt Calista to see her so quiet. Her sister was usually a ball of energy.

Calista tried to pull the suitcase toward the house, but at first, it wouldn't budge. *What in the world is in here?* Calista wondered. She turned and had to use both hands to pull the suitcase forward. It got stuck once on a sidewalk crack, and Calista grunted as she pulled it free.

She gulped as she considered how she'd get it up the stairs. She turned to ask for help, but her mother and aunt had already disappeared inside the house. Molly still stood on the porch, watching Calista as she chewed on her fingers, looking a little lost.

Calista paused, her heart aching at her sister's condition.

"Do you want to help me?" Calista asked, hoping to distract her. "It's the heaviest thing I've ever moved. I could really use your muscles."

Molly smiled at that, flashing the space where her tooth was missing. "Okay," she said quietly. She came over and got on the bottom stair, pushing with all her might as Calista hoisted the bag up, one stair at a time. Calista was literally sweating by the time she got it inside the front door.

She stood the suitcase up in the foyer, catching her breath. Just then, Freya came swinging by to grab the handle of the suitcase. "All right now, I'll take it from here," she said. "Thanks for your help, girls."

She reached into the pocket of her dress and pulled out several butterscotch candies, holding them out to Calista and Molly. Calista thanked her while Molly squealed with delight, taking two and then running to the kitchen to show their mother. Another flash of life. Calista's worry for her sister eased slightly.

When Molly was gone, Calista looked over guiltily at her aunt.

"Oh, yes," Freya said quietly. "I know what you did. And I know why. But we're going to have to fix it, you understand?"

Calista nodded, embarrassed but grateful. Just then, there was a soft knock on the open front door.

"Pardon me," a male voice called.

Calista and her aunt Freya both turned to see Sheriff Mills standing there. Calista's stomach sank. Could this be about last night?

The sheriff took off his hat and bowed his head politely to Calista's aunt. "Nice to see you again, Freya," he added, extra sweet. "I didn't know you were back in town."

Freya looked him over from boot to collar. Calista immediately sensed that they had a long history together, something old, several things unsaid.

"I only just arrived, Justin," Freya said. "I'm hoping you're here to welcome me home."

He laughed. "You know I'm always happy to see you," he said. "But, unfortunately, I'm here on business. Mind if I come in?"

Calista shrank back to the wall, trying to make herself as small as possible. This was definitely about the failed rescue last night. When Calista turned, she saw her father standing on the stairs, his arms crossed over his chest as he listened.

Nora came walking out from the kitchen, wiping her hands on the top of her jeans. "Can I help you, Sheriff?" she asked, brow furrowed.

"Hello, Nora," Sheriff Mills replied. Calista felt a flash of sympathy radiate off him. He'd been the one who came to the house to tell them that Mac had died. Calista knew he was thinking about that moment again.

Freya tilted her head, listening, but also trying to read the situation.

"I'm sorry to just show up like this," Sheriff Mills said, "but I'm not sure if you're aware of the incident last night."

Calista swallowed hard as the sheriff cast a stern glance in her direction. Right about then, she wished she had the ability to evaporate like one of the spirits.

"Incident?" Nora repeated, her voice concerned. "Everything okay?"

"Uh . . ." The sheriff shook his head from side to side as if weighing out his answer. "It was unfortunate," he said. "You see, the Davis boy—"

"The missing one?" Calista's mother asked worriedly.

"No," the sheriff said. "His brother, Wyland Davis? I believe he goes to school with your daughter."

And right then, Calista could feel that her mother knew what was coming next. Nora shot a look at her before placing her hands on her hips, her defenses up.

"Go on," she told Sheriff Mills.

"Well," he said, trying to be tactful, "Calista told Wyland Davis that his brother was out at the marshes, in an old building. We mobilized and searched the entire area, and the only thing standing was an old lookout station. We found nothing. And we spent considerable resources, Nora. A few of our vehicles even got stuck in the mud due to the storm. National news picked it up. And to be frank," he added, fidgeting with the hat in his hand, "it made us look incompetent. That's the story they're running. How we can't find our own boys and that we're turning to local psychics for the answers."

Calista saw her aunt Freya shift with annoyance at the insinuation that being psychic was a bad thing. Her bracelets jingled as she adjusted the grip on her suitcase handle, her knuckles turning white.

"I'm sorry for the trouble," Nora said, her voice tight. "We truly hope you'll be able to find those boys soon."

Sheriff Mills watched her a moment, and then nodded. "We're doing our best," he replied. He turned to Calista. "And as for you," he said, forcing a smile, "our department would appreciate it if you didn't start rumors. Give parents false hope. It doesn't help the situation."

"I didn't—" Calista started to say to defend herself, but her aunt reached back her other hand and gripped Calista's arm to stop her. She closed her mouth. "Yes, sir," Calista said to the sheriff instead, lowering her eyes.

The sheriff shifted in his boots, looking around at the

Wynn women. "I understand the family history," he said, sounding more like an old friend. "I'm not discounting it. It's just . . . times have changed. It's making people nervous. So . . . lower profile, yeah?"

Freya sucked at her front teeth and took a step forward to stop in front of the sheriff. Her presence felt suddenly enormous, filling up the room with confidence and dominance. Calista would love to know how she did that. The sheriff took a step back from her, swallowing hard.

"Thanks for stopping by, Justin," she said coolly. "If you'll excuse me, I'd love to catch up with my family now."

He opened his mouth as if he wanted to apologize, but he stopped himself and nodded instead. "Have a good day, ladies," the sheriff said, slipping his hat back on. He turned and walked out the door.

Freya walked over and closed it behind him before spinning to look back at Calista and her mother.

"I never did like Justin," Mac said from the staircase. "He always tried too hard."

"That man has always tried too hard," Freya said in an echo of Mac, even though she couldn't hear him. Calista felt herself smile a little.

"And what are you grinning about?" Freya asked, startling her. "Not the kind of attention this family needs. You shouldn't have gotten involved with the police. I warned you."

"I didn't mean to," Calista said. "One of the boys, his

older brother is in my class. He came by the house last night to see if I knew anything . . . as a medium."

"There was a boy here last night?" Nora asked, her eyes wide. "A living boy?"

Calista was digging herself deeper. She nodded.

Exasperated, Nora threw up her hands. "What is going on with you?" she asked. "I expect you to be more responsible. Is this because of your thirteenth birthday?"

Calista flinched back from the words, and she could tell her mother immediately regretted them. Again, she smelled mud and rot around the thought.

"I apologize," Nora told her. "I know your father will be . . . I—" She fumbled, unable to say the word *gone*. But Calista heard it in her head anyway.

Your father will be gone.

Freya walked over to stand between them, a calming presence. She looked at Calista.

"I understand it's difficult," Freya told her. "You know I do." She turned to Nora. "Do you mind if I speak with her about this?" she asked. "Get an understanding and hopefully explain a few things."

"Of course," Nora said. "That would honestly be great. She doesn't . . . ." Calista's mother looked at her, a frown pulling at her lips. "She doesn't talk to me about this stuff. She barely talks to me at all anymore."

A lightning strike of hurt shot over to pierce Calista's heart. She hadn't realized her mother felt that way. She knew her mother was lonely, but never considered her own role in that loneliness. She loved her mother, she was protecting her mother. She wasn't trying to isolate her.

"I'll get breakfast started," Nora said quietly, and left to go back in the kitchen.

Calista stood there, feeling guilty. When she looked at Freya, her aunt pressed her lips together in a sympathetic smile.

"It's hard," she said. "I understand how hard it is. Let's go downstairs and chat."

Freya began to lead the way but paused and looked around the house. "You can stay up here, Mac," she said quietly. "I want to talk to her alone." She paused. "And hello, Mother. I hope you're feeling well, darlin'."

From the living room, Calista heard rocking and Grandma Josie tapping her feet again.

16

ALTHOUGH IT HAD taken all of Calista's might to get the suitcase in the house, Freya handled it easily as she worked it down the stairs to the basement. There was a sofa down there, which normally wouldn't be for guests because they might find the séance room too creepy. But for Freya, it was perfect.

After a quick look around, Freya laid her suitcase down in the center of the room and unzipped it. Calista came over to see what was inside, still curious about what could be so heavy.

It was books. In addition to a ridiculous amount of perfectly packed dresses, there were stacks of books, large and small, in the suitcase.

"I brought provisions," Freya said. "Now have a seat. First, I want to talk to you personally before your father and my mother come down here."

Calista did as she was told and sat at the table. The vision of Devon in the chair opposite hers was still in the back of her mind, his feet stuck somewhere. His voice distant and lost.

Freya sat and stretched her hands across the table toward Calista. When Calista placed her palms in hers, she was immediately enveloped in love and warmth—a sense of protection and understanding. It brought tears to her eyes.

"You've been grieving before you've even lost a thing," Freya told her, lowering her head to meet Calista's gaze. "And in the meantime, you're missing out on time with them. I know you don't want to lose your father or your grandmother. I really do." She tugged Calista closer. "But you have to look at it like this: you've had these extra years with your daddy—a true blessing. I want you to appreciate that. Not fearing the ending, but loving what you had."

Tears spilled onto Calista's cheeks regardless. "But . . . I don't want them to go," she said. "I've done everything you said. I stayed strong. I tried to protect Mom and Molly. And now . . . I don't want to lose my dad. I'm not ready."

Tears dripped onto Freya's cheeks, too, and she quickly brushed them away. "Oh, honey," she said. "You've been brave. You have. I . . . I'm sorry I put that on you. Thank you for taking care of your family. And you still will. But your daddy . . . It's time, Callie."

Calista burst into sobs, but Freya patted her arm, gently consoling her. "It's going to be okay," Freya whispered. "You'll get to say goodbye. You'll get to tell him you love him, love him more than anything. You'll have a chance at closure."

Calista closed her eyes, understanding what her aunt was trying to tell her, but stubbornly rejecting it just the same. She didn't want to give up talking to Mac. She didn't want to lose Grandma Josie. And she didn't see why she had to. It wasn't fair.

After a moment, Freya gave Calista's hand a soft squeeze and then pulled back to sit up in her chair. Calista wiped the tears off her face and looked at her aunt, her heart heavy with impending grief.

"I'll be around to talk," Freya added. "And for good measure, I'll stick around past your birthday too. Just to make sure you're all right."

"Really?" Calista asked, the weight lifting slightly. "You'll stay?" That did help. Her aunt had a way of brightening up the place, reminding her of the important parts.

"Really," Freya said, nodding. She straightened her posture. "Now, we have some business to tend to. I'm guessing your grandmother has told you about the curse on our family."

"Oh," Calista said, startled by the topic change. "Yes. She . . . There's been a lot going on in town. And at the house. A spirit boy came to see me, but then another ghost—a woman—destroyed him. She was—"

"Edwina," Freya finished for her. The moment after she spoke the name, Freya said a short Latin phrase, a warding charm to keep her away. Calista had already used a similar phrase in her charm, which seemed to be holding. At least for now.

"Wait," Calista said, curious. "How do you know Edwina, but my father didn't? He was shocked when he heard about the curse."

"Let's just say my gifts manifested differently from your father's," Freya said. "He was gifted in charms and spells, but my mother couldn't really keep any secrets from me." She smiled the knowing smile of someone who had read plenty of minds.

Freya let out a heavy breath, and then got up from the table and went back over to her suitcase. As she squatted down in her heels to gather her books, she looked up at the ceiling. "Mac," she called. "Mother. Come down now. We need to sort through this trouble."

Calista's father and grandmother appeared. Grandma Josie tightened her shawl around her shoulders, smiling softly as she admired her daughter. Mac came over to Calista, examining her tearstained face.

"You all right?" he asked sympathetically, seeming to know the source of Calista's grief. He moved his hand as if to touch her, but stopped short because he couldn't.

Calista nodded, the emotion a little too thick to talk through at that moment. But she would make sure she had a chance to say goodbye, just like Freya suggested. She wouldn't miss that moment with her father. She couldn't live with herself if she didn't get to tell him how much she loved him.

Freya came back over to the table with a pile of books

and dropped them down. She began to sort quickly, pushing through them. "Mom," she said, "which one is it?"

"Tell her to look in *Bindings and Breakfalls*," Grandma Josie told Calista as she came to stand next to her daughter.

"*Bindings and Breakfalls*," Calista said, pointing out the small leather-bound book. All the books in the Wynn family were handwritten, kept in meticulous condition to pass down. But Calista had had no idea that her aunt had so many of them in her possession. Calista had thought they were all in her house. She wondered what more she could learn from them. What if there was a chance to keep her gifts? If so, it might be in one of those books.

"About halfway through," Grandma Josie said, making the motion of turning pages.

"Halfway through," Calista repeated for her aunt.

They watched as Freya found the page she was looking for, and then placed the open book on the table for all to read. "A binding spell," Freya said. "Could this work? Bind her in place as we try to vanquish her?"

Mac seemed to consider it. Grandma Josie walked around the table, reading over Freya's shoulder. But she looked disappointed.

"She's too strong for binding," her grandmother said. She turned to Calista. "She isn't just a spirit."

Calista furrowed her brow. "What does that mean?" she asked.

"She destroyed that boy, turning him into physical ash,"

Grandma Josie said, shaking her head sadly. "I think she's found a way to pierce the veil. Edwina walks in both worlds, the living and the dead."

"Is that possible?" Calista asked, confused by the suggestion.

"What is she saying?" Freya demanded, looking around the room before focusing on Calista. "I need the details to get this right," she reminded her.

"Grandma Josie says that Edwina has found a way to pierce the veil and be in both worlds, alive and dead," Calista told her aunt. "But is that possible?" she asked her immediately after. "Can she be both alive and dead?"

Freya straightened, her throat clicking as she swallowed hard. "Mac," she said into the air. "I need more information."

Calista felt left out of the conversation—the adults were talking—even though she was the medium who had to pass along the messages. She didn't like not being included in the discussion, but at the same time, her aunt had full control of the situation. It gave her a bit of relief.

"How many souls did she collect before her death?" Freya asked, her voice sharp. "Back when she was alive?"

"By my count?" Mac said. "Nine, including Virginia."

"Dad said it was nine, including Aunt Virginia," Calista said quietly, seeing her grandmother flinch at the mention.

Freya's eyes widened and she searched the table, hoping for another answer. "She's too strong," she murmured mostly to herself. "She has three more now—that's twelve.

She . . ." Aunt Freya didn't finish her thought, but Calista could read her overwhelming concern. It frightened her to see her aunt scared.

"She destroyed a spirit," Calista added, drawing her aunt's attention. "A boy's spirit that I summoned. She slashed him with her nails and turned him into ash—on this side of the veil."

Freya nodded solemnly. "Thirteen spirits. Once she's collected them, she'll be stronger than ever." Freya closed her eyes, putting her hand over her forehead as if thinking. "Mom," she said after a moment, keeping her eyes shut, "what does Edwina do next? What does she want?"

Calista turned to her grandmother to hear the answer. Grandma Josie's eyes were glassy with tears.

"She wants Molly," Grandma Josie said.

"No!" Calista shouted, jumping back from them. "Why? She can't have her!" Her voice cracked with fear.

"Your sister is the youngest Wynn girl with a gift," Grandma Josie said. "Yours will be gone soon. And if Edwina can drain what your sister has left . . . there will be no more. Nothing left of the family. And at thirteen souls, she will be restored—stronger than ever. A god on this earth with powers to destroy. She's going to punish the whole town. She's going to kill everyone in Meadowmere."

"What is she saying?" Freya asked, snapping her fingers for Calista to hurry up.

Calista felt sick. She wanted to be strong in front of her

aunt, so as the tears slipped out while she relayed her grand-mother's message, she quickly wiped them away, keeping her voice steady.

"Then we have to stop her," Freya announced. "We can't just try—we *have* to succeed."

"Something happened last night," Calista said.

Freya's expression grew guarded. "With?" she asked.

"Molly," Calista replied, the fear still clinging to her skin. "A demon got through my protection spell and it . . . it possessed Molly. The demon brought a message from Edwina. She was trying to get me to the marshes."

Freya stared at her for a long moment before tightening her jaw. "A demon?" she said. "Well, then. We want to make sure we keep our Molly girl close. It's not easy for a demon outside of our realm to possess a medium. So for the demon to make that kind of effort, Molly must be very powerful indeed. Probably why Edwina wants her so badly."

Freya began going through the other books, looking for a spell or a guide on how to stop Edwina. Two hours passed as they pored over every entry in the Wynn family volumes, every spell, every note. At one point, Calista's mother came down to drop off a coffee for Freya. Nora glanced at the books with a worried expression, but without asking for details, she went back upstairs to be with Molly.

The phone began to ring in the séance room, and both Calista and Freya looked at it.

"Can you grab that?" her aunt asked. "I need to get back to my research."

Calista went over and picked up the phone, bringing it to her ear. "Hello?" she asked.

"I should have known you were a fake," the male voice said, shaking with anger and misery.

"Mr. Winters?" Calista said, struck with guilt. She had never called him back. His fury came through the phone, buried itself in Calista's gut.

She recoiled from the sensation but stayed on the line just the same. She felt she owed him that.

"You sent the rescue teams out into the marshes, wasting their time," Mr. Winters continued. "Time they could have spent looking for my son."

"I'm sorry," Calista said. "It was a mistake. I—"

"You and your family are a mistake," he said, choking on the words. Calista didn't think he meant it; he was angry and lashing out. Lashing out at anyone he could. But it didn't make the words hurt any less.

And she *did* know that his son was dead. She knew it even though he didn't. That unfair and tragic advantage kept her from lashing out in return.

"I'm sorry, Mr. Winters," she said, meaning it. "I really am."

He hiked in a sobbing breath and then he hung up the phone. Calista kept it to her ear for a moment, listening to the dial tone. And then she placed it back on the receiver. She was so sorry.

"This is why we have to keep things to ourselves sometimes," Freya said, having overheard the conversation. "They want us to fix everything, but we can't control reality. We just repeat it. And this time, you were wrong. And you'll be wrong again."

"It hurts," Calista said, her hand over her stomach where she still felt the vibration of pain. "Not being able to tell him—even just knowing," she added. "It hurts to know sometimes."

Freya turned back to look at her niece. "In Louisiana, I got myself in a bit of trouble," she said. "It's all sorted now, but some people, even when you do know the truth, they don't want to hear it." Freya shrugged, saddened. "A wealthy widow, a new love. She didn't like my prediction and her new man certainly didn't either. He was after her money. And when I told her, they tried to accuse *me* of stealing. Can you imagine?" she said, disgusted. "I've never stolen a thing in my life. I had to take the time to send the police an anonymous tip as to where the supposedly stolen items were being hidden. They just so happened to be in Mr. Loverboy's safe-deposit box." She laughed. "But you know us Wynns. Sometimes we just know things. Even when it hurts to know them."

The commiseration helped. Most days, Calista felt all alone among the living—but her aunt understood her. And

Calista felt grown up hearing this story, a secret look into Aunt Freya's mysterious life. She liked being confided in. It made her feel braver.

"Now," Freya added, "there will be more calls—I can hear them ringing already. Until another news story replaces the old, you just let it all slide off your back. Their hateful pills can't hurt you unless you swallow them."

"Okay," Calista said, steadying herself against what felt like an impending attack. "I'll be stronger."

"Good girl," Freya said. She looked back down at the pile of books and sighed deeply. "Now, why don't you run along and help your mother for a while," she said. "She's pretty tense up there, I can feel it."

But the dismissal stung Calista's pride.

Shouldn't I be down here with them, figuring things out? she thought, her feelings hurt. *I am the medium.*

"And bring me down a slice of pie when you get the chance," Freya added with a warm smile.

Calista blinked for a moment, unwilling to abandon the task. She glanced over at her father, who seemed to sense her hesitance, and he shrugged. "It's okay, Callie," he said. "While you're up there, you can check on your sister."

Calista left the séance room, stomping her feet a little louder than necessary on her way up the stairs.

17

AS CALISTA ARRIVED upstairs, she glanced toward the front door and jumped when she saw the silhouette of a person standing on her porch. She looked quickly toward the kitchen, where she could hear her mother talking to Molly. The person outside hadn't even rung the bell.

Calista walked over, and when she peeked out the small window, her heart sped up. It was Wyland Davis.

She spun around out of sight, afraid to talk to him. What if he was there to scream at her just like Mr. Winters had on the phone? What if he hated her after they hadn't found his brother? Calista hadn't meant to mislead him. She truly thought she was helping.

Calista considered getting her mother, letting her send him away. But she didn't want to involve Nora in this any more than she already had. She saw how disappointed her mother had been when the sheriff told her that Calista had been involved in last night's search.

Ultimately, Calista knew she'd have to face up to this herself. Explain as best she could without sinking her family even lower in the eyes of the town. It wasn't like she could ignore Wyland forever—she still had math class with him.

Reluctantly, Calista opened the door. Wyland spun around when she did, looking startled to see her. His eyes were wide, his hands shoved into his coat pockets. He swallowed hard before he spoke.

"I . . . I was going to knock," he said.

Calista stared at him, trying to gauge how he felt. Was he angry? *No*, Calista thought immediately. *No, he's desperately sad.*

Calista looked back into the house, scared her mother would hear them talking. It wasn't lost on her that she kept disobeying her mother's wishes. She didn't mean to—not in a stubborn way. But she had business to handle. Her mother didn't understand.

As Calista stepped out onto the porch, Wyland backed up, chewing nervously on the corner of his lip as Calista closed the door quietly behind her.

"I'm really sorry," she told him, bracing for his reaction. "I really did think the boys were at the marshes."

He shook his head. "No, I'm sorry," he said. "I didn't let you explain before I called my mom . . . I should have checked things out before involving her and the police. I . . . I hear the things that everyone is saying about you now. About your family."

"Like what?" Calista asked, wrapping her arms around herself.

"That you're . . . That you're a fraud." He winced even repeating it. "That you're just trying to make money. But I don't believe that," he added quickly. "And I didn't mean to put you in a spotlight. I'm sorry."

Calista couldn't believe that Wyland was apologizing to her after she had sent him to the marshes on the word of a demon. She didn't think she deserved his kindness, but she would take it. She motioned to the outdoor furniture near the side of the house for them to sit and talk.

"Did they find *anything* at the marsh?" she asked as they walked. "Any clues?"

Wyland eased down in the wicker couch while Calista sat across from him on a chair.

"No," he said. "Seemed that no one had been there in years. Actually, the park ranger told my mother he hadn't even known the tower was still there. Kinda funny, since he's like . . . in charge of it all."

But of course, none of this was funny. His little brother was still missing.

Calista and Wyland sat silently for a few moments. A plane flew low, rattling the windows. This time, Wyland didn't look up at it.

"Do you mind if . . . Can I ask you something?" he said quietly.

"Sure," Calista replied. She was nervous about what he

was going to say. She had no idea what to even expect.

"I know they didn't find anything yesterday," he said. "But I was thinking . . . I still believe you. I know you saw something. Can you tell me what it was?" he asked. "Maybe we need to like, figure out what it really means. Maybe I can help."

Calista sat back in the chair. She wasn't sure she should tell him. She had just had this conversation with her aunt about not revealing too much. And yet . . . Calista really wanted someone to confide in. Someone her own age.

"I probably shouldn't," she told Wyland, looking away. "Besides, it's not . . . It's not going to make you feel better. It might make things worse."

"I still want to know," he said. He sat forward on the couch, moving closer to her as his eyes watched her pleadingly. "Besides," he added, "I feel like you're the only person who understands. The police are tracking leads, talking to neighbors. But there's something more going on. I felt it that day in the classroom, felt the cold around me. It's . . . supernatural." He shook his head. "I know no one would believe that. No one but you."

Calista looked back at her house, anxious that her family might come out and see her talking to Wyland. She began to chew on her thumbnail, deciding what to do.

"Please, Callie," Wyland pleaded. "I just need someone to talk this through with. I just want the truth."

She looked over at him. "I can't talk here," she whispered.

"Can you come back tonight? We could walk to the park. It's just a block that way." She pointed down Marble Lane toward Converse Park. It wasn't much of a playground anymore, the slide rusting, the swings missing the actual seats. But it would be quiet at night.

"Okay," Wyland said eagerly. "Nine o'clock?" he asked.

Calista nodded, her nerves completely shot. How in the world would she keep this secret from her aunt? Freya would definitely be able to tell she was hiding something.

But it also felt kind of exciting. Calista had never had a friend outside of her family. Not a single one her whole life. And there was an aura that came off Wyland. He cared what she thought; he did want to talk to her. He wasn't judging her, not one bit.

Calista felt that he wanted to be her friend, and that maybe, he already was.

"I'll see you tonight," she told him, standing up. He got up too, and they quickly waved at each other before she slipped back inside the house.

When she got inside, Calista waited a moment at the door, listening for the tapping feet of her grandmother in the living room. But her family was wholly distracted—figuring things out without her. But she could contribute too. They'd see that.

So Calista went into the kitchen to fetch her aunt a slice of pie, pretending that nothing was wrong.

❦ ❦ ❦

At dinnertime, Freya came upstairs, pressing her lips into a smile as she saw Calista. She pulled her aside, her hand on her shoulder.

"I doubled the protection spell on this house," her aunt Freya told her. "It'll hold. No vengeful spirits or demons will get through."

Calista nodded, relieved, but also a bit embarrassed that her own spell hadn't been enough to keep them safe. Luckily her aunt was here to make it right. Despite the protection spell, Freya hadn't found anything to use against Edwina beyond keeping her out of the house.

"It's too bad I couldn't lay a protection spell on all four corners of Meadowmere," she said. "But it's too big. Protection spells only work in small spaces."

"And there were no other clues in the books?" Calista asked. Freya glanced away.

"Not yet," she said. Her aunt was impossible to read in that moment. Calista wasn't sure if she was hiding something or if she truly didn't know.

"But we're safe for now?" Calista asked, and her aunt turned back to her.

"Of course," she said. "I'm not going to let anything hurt my girls. And I'm not giving up. We'll figure out how to defeat that Edwina. I can promise you that."

Calista believed her wholeheartedly. Her aunt Freya pulled her into a side hug to drive home the point. Just then, Calista's mother came into the foyer.

"There you are," Nora said to them both. "Dinner's ready." She paused. "Everything good?"

"Always is when I'm home," Freya said without missing a beat. She smiled at Nora and Calista followed suit.

Although they loved Nora, neither of them told her about the vengeful spirit in town. They didn't want to scare her.

The kitchen smelled wonderful as they walked in. As they took their places, Molly, Mac, and Grandma Josie already at the table, Freya looked around at the empty place settings in front of her brother and mother. She seemed to have thoughts on the matter, but Calista watched as she turned her eyes away to look at Calista's mother instead. Aunt Freya paused a moment, studying the bandage still wrapped around Nora's hand. She swallowed hard and picked at her dinner.

"So how's work, honey?" Freya asked her lightly. "Things good?"

Calista's mother set her fork aside and sighed. "Same as ever," she said. "Certainly miss having a bit more freedom, but with Mac being gone . . ." She shrugged sadly. "Me and the girls are making do."

Across the table, Molly was pushing the food around on her plate. She had barely eaten. Calista saw her aunt give Molly a wary glance, but she didn't fuss over her. Instead, she slid another roll in her direction.

Molly smiled and grabbed it before Nora could tell her to take two bites of her broccoli first. Grandma Josie laughed to herself because she used to do the same exact thing for Calista.

Impatiently, Calista watched the clock. Mac and Grandma Josie sat at the table, listening contently as Freya and Nora talked about life in general. It must have been nice for them to see Freya again. It wasn't like they could go visit her in Louisiana.

When they finished eating, Nora got up and began to collect the plates, including the ones in front of Mac and Grandma Josie. Freya's eyes narrowed and she jumped up to help, taking them from Nora's hands.

"Let me get that," Freya said.

As the two women walked to the sink, Calista grabbed her own plate and brought it over.

"Maybe it's time," Freya said to Nora quietly. "Time to stop . . ." She held up the plates. "Move on as a family."

Nora stared back at her, and Calista felt her throat tighten. She didn't think her aunt meant any harm in the suggestion. She might even be right. But Calista took offense to it just the same.

"They're still *here*," Calista snapped. "They are right there, and they sit with us every night."

"Oh, honey," Freya said. She turned back to Calista, startled that she'd overheard the conversation. "I didn't mean anything by that. Of course they are."

Nora kept her comments to herself, looking sad instead. She stacked the dishes in the sink and turned on the water.

But this frustrated Calista more. She wanted her mother to speak up on her dad and grandmother's behalf, even if she couldn't see them. Calista *wanted* her to understand what she'd been going through. It was like she didn't even try.

"It's all right," Grandma Josie said quietly. "Don't get yourself worked up, Callie. It's all right."

Calista looked back at her and felt a ping on her heart. Her grandmother was tired, her face sagging with heavy emotion. Edwina's reappearance had brought up memories of her lost daughter, Virginia. It must have been so hard. She had to relive the tragedy, the tragedy that had marred so much of her life . . . and death.

With a quick glance, Calista checked on her father. But Mac was distracted as he lovingly watched Molly pick at the potatoes on her plate.

He's still here, Calista thought. Freya was wrong. *Even other mediums don't believe what they can't see with their own eyes.*

Would it be the same for her? Tears stung her eyes. "I'm going to my room now," Calista announced before anyone could notice. But as she started to walk away, her mother called her name.

"Callie, can you give your sister a bath for me?" Nora asked. "I want to talk to your aunt for a bit."

"Sure," Calista said, keeping her voice measured. She walked over to put her hand protectively on the back of her sister's head. "Come on, Molly," she said. Obediently, the little girl got out of her chair. She didn't even ask for pie.

Molly still hadn't recovered from the possession. So Calista made it a point to be extra sweet to her. She'd even give her extra bubbles, all the way to the lip of the tub. As they exited the kitchen, Calista looked at the clock on the wall again and saw that it was barely seven. Bath time might be a good distraction until she could head out to meet Wyland.

And then, Calista would do her own research and prove that she had a bigger part to play in protecting her family and Meadowmere.

18

AS MOLLY SPLASHED around in the tub, sloshing tufts of bubbles to the floor, Calista sat with her back against the tiled wall, thinking things over. Her sister seemed to be in a better mood as she coated her dolls in elaborate dresses made of bubbles. She talked in made-up voices as Barbie and Princess Ariel went to prom—decorated fin and all. Of course, Molly was years away from understanding prom, but mediums—they just knew things.

Calista wondered how long it would be before school started again. She didn't *miss* it, exactly. But she missed seeing other people her age. What would the school district do if they never found the missing kids? Would she be studying from home until June? Surely they'd have to make other arrangements before too long.

A soft humming carried around the room, a pretty song that Calista couldn't quite place.

"What's that song?" Calista asked, but when she turned to her sister, she realized that Molly hadn't been the one humming. She sucked in a startled gasp and swung around.

And there, just across the floor at the other corner of the bathtub, was the ghost of a little girl. The child was young— second or third grade, maybe—and wearing a school uniform. She smiled at Calista and waved.

Freya had doubled the protection spell, but it had only been against vengeful spirits. Anything against all spirits might have affected her father and grandmother. Just in case, Calista needed to make sure this spirit was as harmless as she appeared.

"Who are you?" Calista asked, her hand over her heart as she calmed her fright.

"That's Evelyn," Molly answered for her, still playing with her dolls. "She comes by to play sometimes."

Calista turned to her sister, her eyes wide. "You can see her, Molly?"

Her sister laughed. "Obviously," she replied, although she mispronounced the word, *ob-ee-ous-ly*.

Calista looked at the ghost again. The little girl opened her mouth and began to talk, but . . . Calista couldn't hear the words. She sat up straighter, sitting forward.

"I can't hear you," Calista said in alarm.

"She said it's nice to meet you," Molly replied, sounding bored.

Calista looked from her sister to the spirit. It was happening. *Oh, no.* Calista jumped to her feet, panicking. She . . . She was losing her gift. It was really happening.

"Molly, come on," she said, abruptly. "It's time for bed."

"But I'm playing."

"Not right now," Calista told her. "I have some things to do. Let's get your pajamas on." Calista reached to yank the plug out of the drain and Molly whined her protest. Calista got down on her knees next to the tub to look at her sister.

"I'm sorry," Calista said. "Can you please do me this one favor? Next time, I'll let you stay until your hands turn into shriveled little raisins. Extra bath time."

"Promise?" Molly asked suspiciously. Calista nodded. "Okay," Molly replied, still disappointed but at least complying.

Calista wrapped her in a big towel, and then got her sister into her favorite pajamas. She walked her to her room and tucked her into bed.

"You can look at your books for a little bit if you want," Calista said, handing her one of her favorites. "I need to go through some things in the basement. Call out if you need anything. I'll hear you."

"Okay," Molly said, already opening a book with a unicorn on the cover.

Calista left the room, closing the door behind her. She headed directly for the basement.

"Dad," she said along the way, needing to talk to him. "Dad, something is happening. Her voice shook. *What if he doesn't show up?* she thought frantically. *What if he's already gone?*

But when Calista got to the bottom of the stairs, her father was waiting for her. "What's wrong?" he asked. "Is Molly all right?"

"She's fine," Calista said, running her hand anxiously over her hair. "And there was a ghost in the bathroom—a good one, I think. A little girl. But . . . Dad," she added, her mouth pulling downward, "I couldn't hear her. I couldn't hear the ghost when she was talking to Molly." She swallowed hard, still grateful that she could see and hear her father. "It's fading, isn't it? I'm losing my gift."

Mac came to pause in front of her, his expression sympathetic. "That's how it starts," he said. "The old technical difficulties." He offered her a smile, although it held a twinge of sadness.

"I can still hear you," she said.

He nodded. "I'll probably be the last to go," he said. "Me and your grandmother. You're confident with us, know us too well. Pretty sure that curse is going to have to pry us apart."

Calista's eyes stung with tears. "And that's it?" she asked. "It'll just disappear? You'll . . . You'll disappear?"

"I'm sorry," he said, making her despair. "At midnight on your birthday. That's how it happened for all of us."

Calista broke down crying then, and Mac came to sit next to her. He placed his hand over hers even though she couldn't feel it.

"Callie," he said. "I'm always going to be here for you. You're never going to lose me."

"Yes, I will," she sobbed. "I don't want you to go."

Mac sniffled hard, his eyes dripping with tears. "Oh, honey. I don't want to go either. But I'll stay with you, right here, as long as you want."

The words struck her differently this time, even though he'd said them before. She looked up to meet his eyes. Mac's appearance had never changed over the past few years. Even as Calista grew up, her father was the same every day. Same hair, same clothes. No new lines on his face.

"What does that mean?" she asked him, wiping her cheeks. "That you'll stay. Dad . . . are you able to . . . pass on if you want?"

A guilty look flashed across his face. "What does that matter?" he asked. "I'm here. Right with my family, where I'm supposed to be."

It hadn't occurred to Calista that her father could leave. He didn't have any unfinished business; he wasn't lost. He was staying for them. He could be at peace on the other side, but instead he roamed their house, keeping his grieving family company.

The downstairs phone rang, startling Calista. She quickly

pulled herself together to dash over to grab it, not wanting to disturb her family upstairs.

"Hello?" she answered.

"Have you seen him?" a woman's voice asked, tense.

Calista looked around the room before realizing she didn't know who "he" was. "Who is this?" she asked.

"This is Thomas's mother, Sharon," she said. "We met the other day, and I need to know. I need you to tell me. Have you seen my son?" Her voice was raw with grief.

Calista was surprised to hear from her. But she didn't know how to answer her question. At the time, Grandma Josie had thought she should tell her that her son was dead. But after everything that had happened at the marshes, and the sheriff telling her not to get involved, she didn't think that was a good idea. So she lied. She hated lying.

"No," Calista said, closing her eyes. "I haven't seen Thomas."

"That means he's still alive," Sharon said with a desperate hope in her voice. "We can still bring him home."

Calista said nothing, wracked with guilt. It was wrong to give the woman false hope. It was wrong.

"I know that you sent them looking the other night," Sharon said. "Have you seen anything else? Any other clues?"

"No," Calista said sadly. "I'm sorry, but no."

"But you'll keep searching, right?" she asked. "We have to look out for our own, Calista. Don't let this town forget about him. You bring Thomas home to me."

"I'm trying," Calista said, soaked with the woman's grief.

"Thank you," Sharon said, her voice close to the receiver. "I . . . I believe you." And then she hung up.

Calista stood a moment before placing the phone back down. As a medium, you learned to expect that people wouldn't admit to believing in you, even when they did. So it was always a jolt to hear. And in that moment, it was also a little painful. She wanted to bring Thomas home. He deserved that.

When she turned to her father, Calista expected him to scold her for lying, but he didn't. Instead Mac shrugged sadly.

"I know it's a lot," he said. "More than you should have had to take on. I wish there was more I could do to help."

As she stared at him, his appearance wavy through her tears, she wondered, with all these books, all this knowledge between her family, why did she have to lose him?

"We can break the curse," Calista said. "If we destroy Edwina, it might break the curse, right?"

"I don't know about that," Mac said, shaking his head slowly.

"No, we can," Calista said, realizing she sounded as desperate as Thomas's mother had on the phone. "If we destroy Edwina before my birthday, then . . . it'll break the curse. I'll keep my gifts, and you won't disappear from my life again." She flashed him a watery smile, tears dripping onto her cheeks. "We can stay together." Calista wiped hard at the tears, sucking back the sadness as hope filled its place.

Her father pressed his lips together. He said nothing.

"Now help me look through these books," she told him. "There has to be something in here, something that Aunt Freya missed. Whatever it takes, Dad—we're going to break this curse."

He nodded and pointed to one of the thick, leather-bound volumes.

"Let's start there," he said.

19

WHILE HER AUNT and mother were talking privately in the kitchen, and Grandma Josie rocked in her living room chair, Calista and her father spent the time looking through the volumes of books that Freya had brought. But like her aunt earlier, Calista found nothing new that they could use against Edwina. Frustrated, she slammed the books shut and went upstairs, demoralized but undeterred.

By eight forty-five, the house had grown quiet. Nora and Molly were both asleep in their rooms, the house feeling cozy and safe since Freya had arrived. Calista's aunt was in the basement with a cup of warm milk and another slice of pie, still scanning through the volumes of books. Grandma Josie was with her, quietly watching on. Even if Freya couldn't see her, Calista knew that her gran just wanted to be close to her daughter.

With one last look at the time, Calista pulled on a

sweatshirt, laced up her sneakers, and slipped outside without being detected.

The night was cast in shadows of dark gray as the heavy clouds blacked out the stars, a sliver of moon hanging to the right. Calista shivered in the cold air and debated going back inside for a jacket, but she didn't want to be late to meet Wyland.

She was nervous. Calista had never snuck out like this before. But she'd spent her whole life hoping a living person would talk to her. Now she had a chance to not only talk to someone with a beating heart, but also maybe even help find the missing kids. Wyland might have a few clues that he didn't even understand.

And if she could solve this, face down Edwina and beat her, Calista might be able to break her curse. It was a lot of hope to hold on to.

Wyland was waiting at the playground, sitting on one side of the weathered seesaws. His hair was covered in a beanie and he wore a puffer jacket. His bike lay on its side next to the park bench. Wyland waved when he saw Calista approach.

"Hi," Calista called. She went over to sit on the merry-go-round, facing him. "Sorry we couldn't talk at my house. My family isn't too happy with the attention we've been getting lately."

"I understand," Wyland said. "The reporters won't stop

calling my house. My mother cries every time they do."

The reporters could be so intrusive. Calista knew she was lucky they hadn't tracked down her name, at least not yet. She understood that everyone wanted to find the missing kids, but they should have some compassion too. It was shameful.

Calista and Wyland were quiet for a little bit before Calista looked at him again. "It's my birthday soon," she said, although she didn't know why she brought it up. She was about to change the subject when Wyland smiled.

"I didn't know that," he replied. "Happy early birthday."

"It's not happy," Calista said, shaking her head. She twitched her nose at the smell that came along with the thought—wet mud and soot. She regretted even bringing up the topic—it stung like a thorn in her skin.

"Why not?" Wyland asked, surprised. "It's always good to have a birthday."

"Not in my family," she said. "I'm turning thirteen. And when that happens, I won't be able to communicate with spirits anymore. I'll stop seeing ghosts. And . . . talking with my dad. I can see him now but he's . . . he's dead."

"Wow," Wyland said. He cast his gaze down to the ground, taking it in. Then he darted a look at her again. "That's amazing, you know?" he added.

Surprised, Calista turned to him. "Do you think?" She definitely did not expect him to feel that talking to her dead father was cool. Honestly, she thought it might scare him off.

"I wish I could talk to my dad," Wyland admitted. "Jerry is my stepdad." He waved off the words before Calista could comment. "He's been around since I was a baby, so he's *like* my dad. But . . . I wish I could have known my biological father. See what he was like."

"He passed away?" Calista asked.

Wyland nodded, solemn. "Car accident. It was a long time ago."

"I could . . . I could see if he's still around," Calista offered. "See if I could get a sense of him."

Wyland's lips parted in surprise. "You could do that?" he asked, leaning forward.

"I can try," Calista replied. "I mean, I won't summon him or anything. I wouldn't want to pull him away from his afterlife. But if he's wandering, maybe he'll hear us."

"Wow. Okay," Wyland said, sounding both scared and excited. He readjusted his seat on the seesaw to face her completely. "What do I have to do?"

"Here," Calista said, motioning to the side. "Let's move to the grass."

They walked over to the grass area and sat cross-legged across from each other. Calista didn't have all the tools she needed, chalk, sweets, a charm—but she was going to try anyway.

Calista closed her eyes and held out her hands. Wyland

slipped his palms over hers and Calista felt an overwhelming sense of pride. Wyland was proud of who he'd become—or at least, he thought his father would be proud of him.

After clearing her thoughts, Calista said a chant and listened closely. She waited for a signal, a sense of movement. Nothing happened. She repeated the chant, listening. Waiting. But after several minutes, nothing happened. Wyland's dad must have passed on.

Calista felt apologetic as she opened her eyes to look at Wyland again. She pulled back her hands, but he kept his palms out for an extra second, his eyes closed.

"He's not there," she said.

Wyland kept his eyes shut a second longer before looking at her again, disappointment deep in his gaze.

"But that's a good thing," Calista added. "It means he's moved on to the next realm. Trust me, you don't want him wandering the world. Spirits get lost that way." She thought of her own father, wandering their property. Staying, even though he didn't have to. Sadness crept under her skin.

"Can I ask you something and you be honest?" Wyland said, drawing her attention again.

"Sure," Calista replied.

"Do you think . . . Do you think my brother is alive?" Wyland asked.

She thought about it and then nodded her head yes. "I do," Calista said, honestly. "Because if he weren't, I think he would have come to me by now. We're going to find Parker alive. I know it."

She smiled and Wyland matched it.

"I know it, too," he said.

A light breeze blew past them, rustling leaves in the nearby trees and whipping Calista's hair around her face. As she peeled a strand away from her lips, there was an echo of a voice, a call. For a moment, Calista's breath caught as she thought it was Wyland's father coming through after all.

Instead, her stomach dropped when Mac appeared in the grass, his form shimmery this far from the house.

"Dad?" she asked, scrambling to her feet. "What are you doing here?"

"Callie," he said, his voice tinny like a bad connection on a phone line. His form was slightly transparent, showing the street behind him. She'd never seen Mac off their property, not since he'd come back as a ghost. She didn't know how it would affect his spirit.

"*Your* dad's here?" Wyland said, jumping to his feet and darting his eyes around wildly. He sounded scared, but also amazed. Of course, he couldn't see Mac even though Calista's father was three feet in front of him.

"You need to get home, Callie," Mac said, her name reverberating through the air. "It's your sister. You need to get home to Molly!"

Calista's pulse exploded and she began to run without

further explanation. She left Wyland at the park, confused and shaken.

What's wrong with Molly? Calista cried in her head. *Please be okay. Please!*

Panic tore through her body as she ran as fast as she could toward her house. And she was nearly there when she heard her mother's scream.

20

THE SOUND OF her mother screaming shook Calista to the core and she nearly missed the curb, tripping before catching herself with her hand on the sidewalk to break her fall. "Molly," she murmured, terrified as she straightened and stomped quickly up the stairs of the porch.

Calista burst in the front door and looked frantically around the entry. No one was there. She opened her mouth to call out, but then she heard her mother scream again from upstairs.

Taking the steps two at a time, Calista ran for Molly's bedroom. The door was already open. When she got inside, she was hit with a wall of ice, the temperature easily below freezing. There was frost on the window and dresser mirror.

Calista's mother was standing at the second-story window, her hands covering her face as she sobbed. Calista turned and found her aunt next to the empty bed, her phone pressed to her ear.

"Yes," she said as if repeating it. "She's missing, Sheriff. She's gone!" Freya looked up to meet Calista's eyes, wide and fearful.

"No," Calista said, falling back a step. It couldn't be true. There was a protection spell on the house!

Calista's breathing was growing erratic as she tried to catch her breath. She found Grandma Josie sitting in Molly's favorite reading chair, her shawl tight over her shoulders, crying softly. Mac appeared next to Calista.

"Steady your breathing," he told her. "We can't have you passing out right now. This is too important."

Calista tried to do as she was told. She looked over at her father. "What . . . h-happened?" she gasped out.

Before he could say anything, Calista's mother heard her voice and turned in her direction. "Oh, thank God," she cried out, and went over to Calista. She ran right through Mac and embraced her daughter, squeezing her tightly.

"Your sister is missing," Nora said, hugging Calista. She pulled back to look at her, brushing her hair away from her face. "When is the last time you saw her?" she asked, her voice shaking.

"After her bath," Calista said, still confused and overcome with horror. "I . . . I put her to bed after her bath. I'm sorry, Mom." Calista began to cry. "I should have stayed, I'm sorry."

Nora shook her head as if telling Calista it wasn't her

fault. She dried her own tears, pulling herself together. "There was a noise," Nora recounted as if giving testimony. "And then Molly yelled for me. I rushed in, thinking she was having a nightmare. It was so cold. But she was gone. She's not anywhere, Calista," she said, her bloodshot eyes meeting her older daughter's. "Where is your sister?"

"Mom, I don't know," Calista said, still crying. "I don't know."

Freya came over, the phone at her side. "The police are on their way," she said, shell-shocked. When she turned to Calista, they shared the same horrified thought.

The Tall Lady had Molly.

They had searched every inch of the Wynn property, basement to attic and all around. From what the police could put together, it would seem that Molly disappeared into thin air, which of course was impossible. So they assumed that someone had come into the house sometime after nine and snuck the little girl out.

Calista told them that she was at the playground. She considered lying, but it didn't matter now. Nothing mattered other than finding Molly. She should have never left her.

"This is my fault," her aunt murmured to her as they watched the police roam the property. "That spell, it wasn't strong enough. I'm sorry." She closed her fist and brought it to her mouth to hold back her cry.

Calista wasn't angry with her aunt, but she was shocked. She had believed that Freya had the ability to keep them all safe, that she was the adult who was there to save the day. But Edwina was stronger. Calista had never considered that anyone was stronger than her aunt Freya.

Sheriff Mills came to address the family, concluding that the unlocked front door was how the kidnapper had gotten in. Although Calista knew that Edwina had no use for doors, several of the officers cast judgmental stares in her direction. She wished she could hide from them. Then again, part of her felt that she deserved the anger. She should have never left her sister's side.

A female officer with blond hair stopped at the fireplace, looking over the items on the mantle. Although the main part of their house was mostly free of mystical items, the family kept a few charms. The officer reached to pick up a coin, bound in twine and dried roses. She turned it over curiously before Freya walked over to her.

"Put that down," her aunt said. "Our décor is none of your concern."

They stared at each other and Calista could feel the young officer's distaste. She didn't believe in the supernatural and she was irritated, possibly from the search at the marshes that Calista had sent them on the night before.

Grandma Josie hadn't said a word since Calista arrived back home. She looked beside herself, oozing misery. Calista wanted to talk to her, hug her. And then she wanted to know everything about Edwina. Every detail big or small that she could think of. She had to find Molly.

"Calista," Mac said, appearing in front of her and startling her.

Not wanting to let the officer know she was speaking to the dead, Calista tried to cover her startled jump with a cough. She then wandered over to the other side of the room, away from prying stares.

"Did you find something out?" she whispered, hoping her dad had more information.

"Not yet," he said. "But why did you leave the house?"

Calista's cheeks immediately turned red. Afraid others in the room would notice, she pretended to readjust a stack of magazines, busying her hands.

"I was with Parker Davis's brother," she murmured. "I wanted to . . . I wanted to know if he was mad at me for sending him to the marshes. And then, I was hoping he'd have information."

"Did he?" Mac asked, upset, but not necessarily with Calista.

She shook her head no. She moved to refold the blanket from Grandma Josie's chair, looking distracted as she talked to Mac.

Her father sighed, seeming to think things over. "Earlier," he said, "before I went looking for you, I was in the basement with your aunt and grandmother. Suddenly, there was this cold air and I knew there was a presence. I tried to find you, but you were gone. So I went to check on Molly. Just before I got to her room, I knew something was wrong. I burst in, but your sister was already gone from her bed. But I looked out the window, and I saw her."

"You saw Molly?" Calista asked in a hushed whisper.

"No," he said. "I saw Edwina. She was floating outside the window and she . . . she smiled at me." Mac fought back his terror, his anger. "She took her, Callie," he said. "And I was powerless to stop her."

"What do we do?" Calista asked at regular volume, and a few officers turned toward her. She nodded at them and threw up her hands as if the question was rhetorical. She turned her back on the room, pretending to look at an old trinket left years ago. "What do we do?" Calista repeated quietly for her father. "We have to . . ." She choked up. "We have to find Molly."

Calista was devastated. All she wanted was to protect her sister and she had failed. She had failed completely. They all had.

"We will find her," Mac said, sounding sure of it. "There has to be something we can use to track Edwina. Track Molly. We won't rest until we find her, I promise you. We just have to be strong."

"I don't know how strong I am anymore, Dad," Calista

said. "My gifts are fading. My birthday is in two days. What if I—"

"Two days?" Mac said, surprised. "Is it, now? Well, happy birthday, sweetheart."

Calista paused, staring at him. "What are you talking about?" she whispered. "Of course it's my birthday."

Mac looked alarmed at his temporary lapse in knowledge. His mouth opened and snapped shut. He looked around the room. "Oh, dear . . ." he murmured.

Calista took a step closer to her father, her heart racing.

"Dad, are you forgetting stuff?" she asked.

"No," he said, shaking his head. "How could I? I haven't left this house in years."

"You were just at the park," she said, swallowing hard. "You came to find me at the park down the road."

"I did?" he asked, furrowing his brow. Mac put his hand over his forehead. "I . . . I can't seem to recall that."

Calista looked frantically over to her aunt, who caught her eyes and immediately understood that something was wrong. Freya put her hand on the female officer's arm.

"If you'll excuse me," Freya said, now buttery soft. Calista's aunt crossed the room toward her, stepping right into her father without realizing. Freya shivered once and Mac reassembled next to her.

"Dad came to find me at the park," Calista said quietly, still feeling guilty that she had been there in the first place.

"And now he's lost a little bit of his memory."

Freya sighed, concerned. "Well," she said, leaning in so no one could overhear them talk, "Mac, you just stay in the house for a bit. I'm sure it will resolve. No more going out. Not unless you don't plan on coming back."

Calista's aunt looked pointedly at the air around her. It reminded Calista that her father *chose* to be there, meaning he could cross over at any time. Judging by her aunt's tone . . . she seemed to think he should.

"I just want my little girl," Nora pleaded, cutting through the quiet in the room. She was standing with the sheriff, a blanket over her shoulders. Sheriff Mills had a notebook out, his pen scratching on the paper. His eyes were sympathetic.

"We're going to do everything we can, Nora," he said. "I promise you. The governor is going to make a statement soon. Four kids are missing in Meadowmere. They might even bring in the FBI."

"*Four*," Calista repeated to herself. "Four kids, just like I thought."

She should have known better. Her intuition had given her a glimpse into the future, but she had ignored it. And she had trusted a protection spell instead of staying by her sister's side. She'd never forgive herself if she couldn't save her sister. She couldn't survive without Molly.

More tears threatened to fall, and even though Calista tried to fight them back, she couldn't stop from crying. Soon, her crying turned into sobs and her mother rushed over to wrap the blanket around Calista's shoulders too, pulling her into a tight hug.

"We're going to find her," her mother said. "And your father's going to help. Your gran and aunt, too. We're going to get her back."

But Nora sounded more desperate than hopeful. As Calista lifted her wet eyes, she saw her grandmother watching them from across the room. Heartbroken.

21

CALISTA STAYED WITH her mother until the police left, the house submerged in eerie silence once they were gone. Several neighbors had come by in the chaos, giving statements that they'd seen Calista running back to the house, looking frightened. Heard Nora scream. But no one saw Molly leaving the house.

It was close to two a.m. when Calista's mother was finally ready to go lie down, her face swollen from crying. Calista was worn out with exhaustion, fear. Grief. She didn't know what to tell her mother about what had happened; she didn't have the answers. Although the sheriff mentioned the unlocked door, Calista knew that had nothing to do with her sister's disappearance. And she suspected her mother knew the same.

After helping her mother to bed, Calista left Nora's room. She went out to the living room, where her aunt was drinking a cup of tea, staring at the unlit fireplace. Mac stood at the mantle while Grandma Josie rocked in her chair, the sound of rhythmic tapping filling the room. The entire world felt surreal, like the edges of a nightmare that kept threatening to pull you back under.

"We don't have much time," Freya said without looking over. "After your birthday, you won't be able to communicate anymore. That means . . . if something happens to Molly . . ." Her voice cracked. "We might never know. She might never find you."

Calista bit back the sob that threatened to escape at those words. She had to be strong now. And to force it, she balled her hands into fists at her sides.

But at that moment, her aunt fumbled to set her teacup back on its saucer. Then Freya covered her face with both palms and completely fell apart. The sight of it was startling, her incredibly brave aunt crying—it just wasn't possible. Then again, Freya hadn't thought it was possible for Edwina to get her sister either. Now nothing was right. And until they had Molly, it never would be again. It seemed so long ago that Calista had felt grown up enough to deal with adult problems. She didn't want to be the adult now. She wanted someone who knew what to do.

Calista went over to kneel next to her aunt's chair, resting her hand on her leg until her aunt gripped it, squeezing it for support. Calista stayed with her aunt as she got out all the emotion she could. A faucet of pain flowing over both of them.

And when she finished, pulling out her handkerchief to dry her eyes, Grandma Josie's voice echoed in the room.

"Now let's get started," she said impatiently. "We're going to summon that awful old witch and demand she release our baby."

Calista's heart jumped into her throat as she swung around to look at Grandma Josie. The old woman was standing in the doorway, her face set in determination.

"Are you serious?" Calista asked, shocked. "You want to *summon* Edwina? Here?"

"We don't have any other choice," she replied, pressing her lips tightly together.

"Is that my mother?" Freya asked, sitting up and looking around. "Ask her if she's lost her mind. We can't let that woman near another Wynn."

"She said there's no choice," Calista said, looking back at her aunt. But Freya's expression was fraught with concern.

"I can't protect you," Freya said, reaching to place her hand on Calista's shoulder. Then she turned toward the door. "Mom, I can't keep her safe from the spirit. She got through my spell. We are completely exposed here."

Calista's eyes widened with fright. She hadn't considered that Edwina could come back to harm any of them. She was obviously more powerful than any of them had anticipated.

"Calista can protect herself," Grandma Josie said. "And besides, if Edwina wanted her, she would have taken her the other night."

Calista gulped, unsure if her grandmother's thought made her feel any better about her situation.

"But she's almost out of time," Grandma Josie added, finding Calista's gaze. Tears shone in her eyes. "Your father told me your gifts are fading. It's now or never, child. Your sister's life is at stake."

Calista knew that her grandmother was scared. She turned to look at Mac to gauge his reaction. He was chewing on his lip, as if searching for softer words, something reassuring to say. But Calista knew her grandmother was right. If she didn't act, Molly could die.

Calista turned to her aunt. "Will you help me prepare?"

"Oh, honey," Freya said. Calista felt the concern pouring from her aunt's soul. But after a moment, it turned to resignation. Right was right. She knew they had to stop Edwina tonight.

With her mother safely in bed and the house locked up tightly, Calista and the rest of her family went downstairs into the séance room. While Calista collected items and placed them strategically on the table, Freya flipped through books and used chalk to mark different binding phrases on the table, notes for Calista to use during the summoning.

"We're just going to use them all," Freya said as she worked. "We will literally throw the entire book at her."

"So how do we do it? What's the plan?" Calista asked, handing her aunt a coin from the box of charged objects.

"We are going to summon her, conjure her, and then

bind her long enough to kill her," Freya said. She paused to look at Calista. "We have to kill her, Callie. Now, here." She reached into a hidden pocket in her suitcase and pulled out a small dagger. Calista's eyes widened.

"You brought a knife?" Calista asked, shocked.

"Never leave home without a backup plan," Freya murmured, and put the knife beside her chair. "Once Edwina is bound, I'll be able to see her in this veil. And then, I'll end her."

"That'll . . . work?" Calista asked, looking at where the knife was hidden.

"Yes," Freya said confidently. She turned to Calista. "But we need to find out where she's keeping your sister. Once we do, and once she's in our binding on this side of the veil, I'll plunge the dagger into her heart. It's an object charged by the blood moon and it'll send her where she belongs, permanently. Just don't give her a chance to escape."

"I won't," Calista promised.

After they all sat down at the table, Freya outstretched her hand and Calista took it, feeling her aunt's power intertwine with hers. Although Freya wasn't a medium anymore, her power still pulsed strongly in her veins. Calista had never felt anything so alive, so elemental. She was so glad her aunt was with her. They were about to get Molly back. End this nightmare. Maybe even end this curse.

Freya drew in a deep breath, stretching herself tall as her eyes fluttered shut. "And now we begin," she said.

The room felt suddenly smaller as Calista focused. Freya began the summoning, but the words and phrasing were more difficult than what Calista was used to. As Freya spoke, certain Latin words were pitched higher, creating a chant that began in the diaphragm, vibrated in the throat. Calista put all her confidence into speaking the sounds aloud. She felt them shake her soul.

"Appare," Freya whispered. "Appear."

Suddenly, the candles on the table blew out, submerging the room in darkness. Calista dropped her aunt's hand quickly to relight them. She scratched the match against the igniter. When she did, Edwina stood across from her at the end of the table.

Calista shivered in the sudden burst of icy air that came along with the Tall Lady, the smell of rot and mud. The malice and hatred.

"She's here," Freya said, her voice surrounded in puffs of white smoke.

"She is," Calista agreed, lighting the candle but never taking her eyes off Edwina. When the room was illuminated again, Calista put the matches down and gripped her aunt's hand. Calista could feel her shaking.

"Give us Molly," Calista told Edwina, her voice clear and brave. "I want my sister."

Edwina laughed, a sickening sound that made Calista's ears pop.

"I think not," the hateful spirit said. "For such a little thing, she is quite powerful. She reminds me of someone." Edwina smiled, flashing her sharp teeth. Then she turned to find Grandma Josie at the table.

"Their power is not yours," Grandma Josie said angrily. "You are damned, and you know it!"

Edwina had been comparing Molly to her aunt Virginia— her dead aunt Virginia. Calista's breathing became uneven, but her aunt squeezed her fingers, as if sensing that fear and offering her strength.

"What do you know of power?" Edwina asked Grandma Josie. "You stole mine."

"I did no such thing," Grandma Josie shot back, unafraid. "You harmed those children and the town put you in the ground. *I* didn't take anything."

"But it was your words that condemned me," Edwina said. "Your jealousy."

"The darkness in your heart is blinding you to the truth," Grandma Josie told her. "You brought it all on yourself, Edwina. They would have found you eventually."

Edwina lowered her head but kept her eyes trained on Calista's grandmother, hatred burning in them brightly. Calista thought her grandmother was right. Edwina blamed the Wynns, but it was clear that this woman had been wicked long before her grandmother reported what she'd done. And dying that way, with that kind of malice, would only intensify that wickedness.

Calista knew in that moment that Edwina's spirit wanted only one thing—to destroy the Wynn family entirely. To destroy *everything*.

Without waiting for advice, Calista began chanting the binding spells that her aunt had written on the table for her earlier. They were powerful, and Calista felt a surge of energy from all around her. She closed her eyes as she drew it in, saying the Latin phrases without pause, every syllable strong and forceful. She heard Edwina hiss in pain at the end of the table.

Encouraged, Calista looked at Edwina again and found the spirit's hands were palm down on the table, as if stuck there. The binding was working! Edwina's form shimmered, being pulled across the veil in a weakened physical form. Calista saw her aunt reach down for her dagger. Another minute and Freya would be able to attack the witch.

"Tell me where Molly is," Calista demanded of the spirit. "Where are you keeping my sister?"

Edwina bared her teeth, the table beginning to shake. "I will destroy all of you," Edwina said slowly, her eyes growing wide and round. "You will never see your sister again."

Rage tore through Calista. She stood up from the table, dropping her aunt's fingers as she raised her own hands at her sides. The energy in the room was pulsing with pain and power. Thick with darkness—Calista could feel it. Her emotions were becoming too much. Her hair began to float in the air; her skin felt electric. Her eyes faded into black.

She hated this woman—this witch.

"Give me my sister!" Calista shouted at Edwina, the glass in the room rattling at the power in her voice. Her veins felt like they were pulsing with fire. "Give me Molly!"

"I'm starting to see her," Freya murmured. "Bring her through!"

But Calista didn't turn to her aunt. She focused on Edwina and watched the spirit wince with pain, her hands held fast to the table. She wanted to hurt her. She wanted to make her pay.

Wind began to swirl in the room, pushing items through the air. There was a smell of burning hair, burning hair and sulfur, acrid and stomach-turning. Calista couldn't stop—the hate was flowing into her freely, giving her power she'd never had before.

"Calista . . . ," Freya warned, looking at her. She sounded frightened. "Stop."

"Never," she replied, raising her hands higher as invisible lashes pulled Edwina closer to the table, binding her.

"You're drawing on *her* abilities," Grandma Josie said urgently, close to Calista's ear. "Stop, Callie. You don't want that kind of energy. You don't want that curse."

"I *want* to destroy her," Calista growled, even as tears slipped from her eyes. She was filled with so much anger. It was a shadow on her heart, coating all of her vessels in that black oil. Dark power.

"Callie, stop," Mac said, appearing at her side. "Please! Edwina is already taking your gifts; don't let her take your soul, too."

Calista met his eyes for a moment, but her hatred was still so strong. This was the only remedy for her fear and helplessness. This was true power—destructive, unforgiving.

Despite her father's pleas, Calista turned back to Edwina and bared her teeth, tightening the restraints until they began to disfigure the witch's hands. At Edwina's cry of pain, Calista felt another surge of power—icy and sharp with its misery.

"Please, Callie girl," Mac murmured, desperate. "You see what dark magic has done to Edwina. That's not you. That can never be you. You're too special to me. To us. Please," he begged. "Let go. Come back to us. We need you. Molly needs you."

Mac reached up to put his hand next to Calista's cheek, hovering there, but unable to touch her. And yet, she could feel the warmth of his love, a concentrated stream of sunlight. And she yearned for it. Despite the sharp edges of hatred cutting into her, the love from her family, her love for them, chased away the anger. It chased it clear away the moment she thought about her sister. And just like that, the connection to the dark forces in her mind were severed with a *snap*.

Calista's entire body seemed to gasp. She fell back in

her seat, surrounded by her family and their love. Her heart beat erratically, her skin stinging from the effects of Edwina's power.

When Calista looked across the table at Edwina again, the spirit grinned. For a moment, the evil spirit was still held in the spell, although her edges were thinning and beginning to dissipate. Then the Tall Lady lifted up her hands from the table and shook them. There were deep red marks twisted around her wrists like she'd been tied up, but they quickly faded.

"That's what you Wynns always lacked," Edwina said, straightening up. "Dedication."

Calista was trying to catch her breath. "I don't want to be like you," she managed to gasp out. "I don't want to be a monster."

"Little girl," Edwina spat, her voice poisonous, "you can't stop me. None of you can. You're all weak and—"

With a sudden burst of chaotic energy, Freya raised her dagger, ready to pounce. But Edwina saw her first, and gripped the underside of the table to flip it. When she did, Calista went sailing backward in her chair, the wind knocked out of her as her back banged against the floor.

Calista's aunt screamed as the heavy table tilted to the side in midair, knocking Freya off her chair before landing solidly on top of her, the dagger skittering across the room.

The candles rolled off the table onto the floor. One

bowled toward the curtains, the fire from its wick licking out at the fabric.

Calista jumped to her feet, wincing at the pain she felt in her back, and raced over to turn on the overhead light. She stomped out the candle before the curtains could catch fire.

She spun to face Edwina, but the Tall Lady was gone. A cloud of black soot hung in the air where she had stood.

Freya moaned from the floor. Immediately, Calista ran over and dropped to her knees next to her aunt, taking stock of her condition. Freya's shoulder was at an odd angle, her right arm pinned. The heavy wood table rested on her chest, and Freya motioned with her free arm that she couldn't breathe. She was being crushed.

Calista tried to move the table, but it wouldn't budge. Her aunt was dying and she couldn't help her. She grew more panicked, terrified. The table was too heavy!

"Mom!" Calista screamed as loud as she could as she continued to try to lift the table. "Mom, help!" she added.

Frantically, Calista looked around the room for something to use as leverage. The sound of her mother's footsteps racing down the stairs echoed around her. "We're in the basement!" Calista screamed. "Help!"

Calista's aunt Freya was turning a purplish color, slapping the table with her palm as if begging for it to be moved. Her eyes were starting to bulge out slightly.

Calista needed to save her aunt and fought desperately

to do just that, but nothing was helping. Calista was crying, screaming as her mother got to the bottom of the stairs.

"Oh, no!" Nora cried out when she saw the wreckage in the room. "Freya!"

Calista's mother raced to where the table had been tipped over, taking quick stock of the situation. She directed Calista.

"Grab it here," Nora commanded, pointing to one edge of the table near the heavy leg. "Now use your knees," she added. "As we lift, you push it to the side. We need to get it off her chest."

Mac paced frantically behind them, and Grandma Josie stood shocked, her hand over her mouth, eyes damp with tears.

Calista followed her mother's suggestion. With all her might, she lifted the corner of the table alongside her mother. It raised a few inches, and Freya took a gasp of air before wincing in pain. The table was so heavy, and Calista wasn't sure she could hold it. But then her mother leaned toward her, her eyes determined.

"Don't you set that table down, Calista Wynn," she said sternly. "You're going to hold it just like this. All on your own while I slide Freya out. On the count of three, you understand?"

Calista grunted, using every ounce of strength that she had. She sputtered out, "One, two, three!"

Nora let go and the weight of the table almost buckled

Calista over, but she held on, her arms shaking. She screamed again to force adrenaline through her body.

Immediately, Calista's mother reached down to grab Freya under the arms, making her cry out in pain. Nora pulled her quickly from under the table, falling backward with her body the moment it was clear.

"Got her," Nora called.

Calista dropped the table and the weight of it pulled her down on top of it. She lay there for a moment, trying to catch her breath. Her arms felt loose, like overstretched rubber bands.

"Call 9-1-1," Nora said in between gasps. "Tell them we need an ambulance." She reached down to brush Freya's hair away from her forehead. "I'm here, honey," she whispered to her.

Calista saw that her aunt was unconscious, blood seeping from the corner of her mouth. Calista didn't know if she'd be okay. And she was scared to look around, afraid . . . afraid she'd see her aunt's ghost.

22

IT WAS NOT until almost ten the next morning that Calista got a call from the hospital. Her mother had gone with Freya in the ambulance, insisting that Calista wait at the house with a neighbor in case Molly showed up.

The neighbor, Mrs. Dominguez, handed the phone to Calista with a comforting smile. "It's your mother," she said, and left to go into the kitchen to give her some privacy.

Calista sat on the couch while Grandma Josie waited in her chair, her feet tapping impatiently on the wood. Mac stood at the fireplace.

"How is she?" Calista asked before her mother could say a word. "Please tell me she'll be okay." Her breath was caught up in her throat as she anticipated her mother's next words.

"Your aunt just got out of surgery," Nora said, sounding exhausted. "She isn't awake yet, but she needed to be sedated. Her collarbone, arm, and several ribs are broken."

Nora paused. "But she's going to be okay. She's just not going anywhere for a couple of days. Doctor's orders."

Calista sniffled just as tears began to gather. Her aunt Freya had gotten hurt. Formidable, powerful, all-knowing Freya. How could this have happened? What were they supposed to do now?

"Any news there?" Nora asked, her voice tight. "Has the sheriff come by? Any neighbors?"

She was talking about Molly. But there had been nothing new. And horridly, Calista knew there would be nothing. Not unless Edwina willed it so.

"No," Calista replied, miserable. "It's been quiet here."

Nora breathed for a moment, the sound soft over the phone. "And before that?" she asked with a knowing tone. "Whatever you were doing in the basement, did you find your sister? Just tell me the truth—did you . . . did you *see* Molly?"

"No," Calista said. "She's alive. And I'm going to find her, Mom. I won't give up. I promise you"—her voice cracked— "I'll never give up. I'm going to bring Molly home."

"I need you to be careful, Callie," Nora whispered, desperate. "I can't lose you, too."

Calista didn't answer because she wasn't sure she could promise that. She would go as far as she needed to save her sister. No matter what her father said, in the end, if only one Wynn girl survived, then so be it.

"I'll be heading home now," Nora said, sniffling back her tears. "Please let Mrs. Dominguez know I'm on my way."

Calista hung up and told the neighbor that her mother would be there soon. Then she went back to the séance room to survey the damage. In the air was the smell of soot and melted candle wax. The table was still on its side, papers strewn about from damaged books. Calista tried to think of any indication she'd gotten from Edwina as to where she was holding her sister. There had to be a clue they'd missed. She couldn't think of anything.

Edwina wanted to destroy her family and Calista felt powerless to stop it. She went over and sat on the couch, alone and afraid. Grandma Josie appeared in the room along with her father. They stayed with Calista while she cried, no one needing to say a word.

After her mother arrived home, Calista sat at the kitchen table with her. The sheriff popped by with a few more questions along with several other officers. They walked the property once more, but had no updates on Molly. Calista's mother ignored the reporters who were constantly calling the house. Nora wanted to unplug the phone but couldn't risk missing an update or even a call from Molly.

As the day slid into evening, Calista found herself standing outside her sister's bedroom. She opened the door, hoping to find Molly playing with her dolls on the rug. But, of course, the room was empty. It wasn't cold anymore, not like the night before. The darkened window was locked, Molly's bed still unmade. There was a latex glove left behind on the dresser from when the officers had searched the room. Calista went over to grab it, not wanting to leave it in her sister's room. It didn't belong. It was a reminder of how terribly wrong the world had become.

She missed Molly so much. It felt like a hole in her chest, an entire piece of her torn away. She imagined her mother felt the same. Or worse.

It reminded her of when her father died. That initial grief before Mac appeared to her shortly after. While her mother was still sobbing at the door and Grandma Josie's ghost cried softly in her chair, Calista had stood in the living room, clutching her gut like she might throw up. And then suddenly, Mac appeared at the fireplace, a bit confused before fixing his eyes on Calista and smiling. "I'm here, Callie girl," he said. "Don't cry, I'm here."

Calista never really had to grieve her father. She didn't have to grieve Grandma Josie, either. But if she didn't find Molly by tomorrow night . . . If she didn't find her sister by tomorrow night before her gift left her completely, she would never see Molly again. Her sister would be lost forever, even her soul.

Slowly, Calista backed out of Molly's room and quietly closed the door. She was tired—she hadn't slept in over twenty-four hours. She knew she'd need the rest. Tomorrow was her last day to make it right. Somehow.

23

CALISTA WOKE UP at close to ten in the morning, her eyes still swollen from crying the day before. It took a minute for the weight of the world to crash down around her. Her sister was missing. This was the last day with her gift—her father and grandmother. It was an explosion of pain and grief.

After changing clothes and brushing her teeth, Calista went downstairs and found her mother on the couch, staring expectantly out the front window. She was waiting for Molly to run up the walkway, out of breath as she told them about her latest adventure. Safe and sound, back at home. But Molly didn't come home. Molly was missing.

Calista and her mother went through the day in a haze. Nora made herself cups of tea that she forgot to drink, made phone calls that would end in her sobbing on the line. Mac sat on the staircase, his face in his hands as Grandma Josie rocked slowly in her chair.

Freya was still in the hospital. Strong, smart Freya who always knew what to do. Calista couldn't help but feel like the moment her aunt was attacked . . . they had lost. Edwina had beaten her aunt so easily, and the witch was right. Calista was no match for her either.

Every tick of the clock filled her with more dread. They were running out of time. Calista didn't know what to do; she waited for a sign. A murmur from a ghost or a call from her sister.

After hours of silence, Calista went to her bedroom to think. As the sun began to set, she was startled when she heard a pebble hit her window. She quickly got up and went over to look out, unsurprised when she found Wyland there. He waved for her to come down.

While her mother was in the kitchen talking on the phone to a neighbor, her father and grandmother standing close to listen, Calista slipped outside and met Wyland in the grass. He looked beside himself with worry.

"How are you?" he asked. "Any news on Molly . . . or my brother?"

She shook her head no. "But . . ." She stopped.

"Tell me," he said, taking a step closer. "Please just tell me everything."

Normally, Calista would have held back. But the secrets didn't seem to matter anymore. None of it mattered if Molly was gone. So she took a breath and told Wyland everything.

"Last night I summoned the spirit who took them," Calista

said. "She's a vengeful spirit, an evil spirit who hates my family, hates this whole town. We tried to find where she was keeping them, and then kill her, but we couldn't defeat her," Calista added miserably. "She was too powerful. She . . . She ended up hurting my aunt really badly. Put her in the hospital." Calista's eyes welled up. "And at midnight," she added, "I'm going to lose my father and grandmother all over again. I'm going to lose my sister forever."

Calista began to cry, wishing she could hold back the pain. But it was too much.

A bit awkwardly, Wyland reached over to pat her shoulder and then slowly pulled her into a hug. "I'm sorry," he whispered. "I wish I knew how to help. I just . . . I want to find Parker and Molly and bring them back home with us."

Calista straightened and wiped the tears off her cheeks. She was embarrassed, but crying a little had helped clear her head. She blinked as she pulled herself together.

Across from her, Wyland looked around the street as if searching for an alternative way to find their siblings. Then he turned back to Calista.

"We have until midnight, right?" he asked. When Calista nodded, his eyes flashed with hope. "Then let's use every last second," he said. "What are our options? What can you do?"

Calista thought about it. "We could search in the physical world," she said. "If we can find the kids, it might strip Edwina of some of her power. Stop her from bringing that power into our side of the veil. But I don't know where to look, Wyland," she added, still feeling defeated.

"There are the marshes," he said, thinking over the options. "But the police have already searched the lookout station next to Black Water Road. And there was nothing else in the marshes, everything has sunken into the mud."

Into the mud. That was true—just like Edwina's old shack, almost everything in the marshes had been reclaimed by the mud. Sucked below the surface.

Suddenly, Calista remembered what the demon had told her. The missing kids were in a small building, little more than four walls and tragedy.

Tragedy? What did that mean? She turned to Wyland.

"What if there was another building?" she asked him. "What if the police checked the wrong one?"

Wyland furrowed his brow. "There is no other build-ing," he said. "I rode my bike out there, just to check again. But . . . nothing was there. Literally, nothing else standing. Just the one lookout tower near the highway."

That highway had been there for years, one of the first things built in Meadowmere. Built on solid land. It wasn't sinking. It . . .

Calista paused, an idea forming. Solid land . . . where things didn't sink. Four walls and tragedy.

Calista looked hopefully at Wyland and he matched her energy, ready to hear what she was about to say. Instead, she glanced back at her house to check for her mother. When she didn't see her, she grabbed Wyland by the shirtsleeve.

"Come on," she said, tugging him toward the door to the séance room. She needed Grandma Josie's books.

"Where are we going?" Wyland asked, but dutifully followed.

Calista unlatched the basement entrance, and then she and Wyland went inside. When she clicked on the overhead light, Wyland let out a low whistle.

"Whoa," he said, looking around. "What happened in here?"

"This is where I summoned the witch who has our siblings," Calista said, as if it was completely normal. She pointed toward a blackened circle burned into the floor. "She was right there." Wyland stared at the spot a moment and then ran his hand over his hair. He looked a bit frightened.

"Grandma Josie," Calista called into the air as she walked over to the shelves. "Dad. I need you both."

Wyland stayed by the door, sliding his hands into the pockets of his jeans. He chewed nervously on his lip as Calista spoke to her dead family members.

"What's going on?" Mac asked Calista when he appeared in the room. His eyes were wide with worry. "Are you okay?" He looked over and noticed Wyland. "Oh," he added in surprise.

Calista was at the shelf, sorting through the volumes of Wynn history books. They were now scattered and out of order, but she was searching for one in particular—the one with the section on lost souls. When she was talking with Wyland, she had remembered something from when she looked through it earlier in the week with her grandmother.

The map of the marshes.

The demon had told Calista that the missing kids were in a small building, and there was only one with the kind of tragedy that a demon would recognize—Edwina's old shack. Not only had town children been lost there, Edwina herself had been murdered within the walls. But Calista's grandmother had told her that Edwina's home was long gone, sucked back into the mud of the marshes.

"I think they were looking in the wrong place," Calista said with a surge of hope and absolute fear. "Edwina's house was in the marshes—but it sank. What if it's not entirely gone? Or what if part of it remains? The kids could be there, under the mud. Hidden."

Mac nodded and pointed to the books as if telling her to keep looking. "That's good thinking, Callie. You might be on to something."

"Wait," Wyland said, overhearing Calista. "Are you saying the kids are *buried*?" Terror clung to his words as he ran over to meet her at the shelf. "Calista, are they still alive?"

"I don't know," she said honestly, not willing to lie anymore. "But I believe Parker and Molly are holding on. Which is why we have to get to them."

"Should I . . . Should I call the police?" Wyland asked, looking around helplessly.

"No," Calista said. "We can't involve them. Not yet. They'll only slow us down. Besides, how is the sheriff going to deal with an evil spirit?"

Grandma Josie appeared and walked over to where Calista was standing. She ran her eyes across the disheveled stack of books before reaching out a shaky finger toward the one Calista was looking for.

"Thank you, Gran," she said. Calista grabbed the book and flipped through until she found the loose page with the map. X marked the spot.

"Right there," Grandma Josie said. "That's where Edwina used to live. But it's surely below the earth now."

"That's where they are," Calista said breathlessly. She could sense it—her intuition was screaming out to her. She smelled the wet earth, the rotting wood. And mixed among them, the soft scent of Molly's favorite bubble bath. Calista showed the map to Wyland, her courage growing with each second.

"I don't understand," Wyland said, pointing to the place on the map that she'd indicated. "This is where they are? But I'm telling you, it's not there anymore," he added. "Nothing is. So what do we do? Dig it up?"

Calista considered the question. Her grandmother had told her that Edwina walked on both sides of the veil. She was real enough to take living children; she was dead enough to disappear into the ether. What if her home was the same—existing in two places?

She tucked the map into her pocket.

"I don't think we're going to have to dig," Calista told him. "She had to get the kids in there, right? That means there's a way inside. And I can find it," she said, nodding. "Places like that, ones that are so steeped in tragedy? They pulse with energy, the same energy that Edwina has been drawing on. It was her home. It's still her home."

"That's what kept her tethered to this realm," Grandma Josie said, realizing. "The house was Edwina's portal between the veils while she grew stronger—a crossing point on both sides, a fixed object between worlds. You have to go there," Grandma Josie added, even though Calista could see how much she disliked the idea. "Edwina will have her thirteenth soul—our Molly. And after that, she'll be unstoppable."

"I know," Calista replied, nodding. "I'm going to end her, end this curse forever." She turned to Wyland. "Are you willing to help me kill an evil spirit?"

Wyland paused a good, long second. "Honestly, it sounds like a really bad idea," he said seriously. Then he smiled. "But I have to admit, you're kind of good at figuring this stuff out. Scary good. So, yeah. Let's go save everybody. I'm in."

"Great," she said with relief. "Now help me find my moon rocks."

Calista and Wyland dashed around the room, gathering supplies: a few coins, rocks, and some chalk. But when Calista bent down to pick up the matches from the floor, she noticed Aunt Freya's dagger slid half under a chair. Calista stared at it, intimidated by the sharp blade. Freya had told her it could vanquish Edwina. And Aunt Freya was rarely wrong. Calista remembered the chant they had used to summon the Tall Lady the night before. Maybe she could make the plan work this time. Call Edwina into their veil as a bound spirit before plunging the blade into her heart.

Intense, but it might work.

While Wyland was distracted, Calista grabbed the knife off the floor and went over to the closet to pull out a heavy coat, slipping the dagger into the inside pocket. Calista then grabbed two flashlights and handed one to Wyland.

At the door to the outside, she paused to look up at the ceiling, imagining her mother in the kitchen on the phone. Nora would be struck down with worry when she realized Calista was gone. But she couldn't tell her mother and risk being stopped. She had to bring Molly home. All that mattered in the world was saving her little sister.

"I'm coming with you," Mac said, appearing in front of the door. His face was set in determination.

"You can't," Calista replied. "Your memories will fade."

"Then you'll just have to tell them back to me," he replied.

"No," Calista said, shaking her head. "I may be losing you, Dad—but I won't take you from Molly too. When we get her back, she's going to need you. And she deserves to know you like I do." Her voice choked up, but she quickly cleared her throat. She was taking control of the situation.

Calista was the person her family needed, just like her aunt had told her years ago. There was no time for grief. This was her time to be strong. "I need you to stay here and watch after Mom," she told her father definitively.

"Callie," Mac said, but she walked right through him.

Calista got out the door with Wyland close behind. Her heart tugged for her to go back to her dad, but she pushed the emotion aside. She and Wyland quietly made their way to the shed on the side of the house, where Calista extracted her bike from the lawn equipment. The tires were low, but they'd work for now.

She and Wyland didn't have a moment to spare. As Calista got on her bike, Wyland jogged over to grab his from the front lawn. They both took off down Marble Lane, heading for the marshes of Meadowmere.

The most dangerous place in all of town.

24

CALISTA WAS OUT of breath as they approached the entrance to the marshlands. The sky had darkened completely on their journey, but neither Calista nor Wyland had turned on their flashlights. Not yet. Better to preserve the batteries instead.

With her bike tires low, the ride had been tougher than Calista anticipated. Her forehead was damp with sweat and she was happy to drop the bike on the gravel road as the path narrowed through the marshes. Wyland set his bike next to hers and the two surveyed the area.

Frogs were croaking all around. Crickets hummed and the reeds swayed in the soft wind. The temperature in this area was at least ten degrees cooler, and Calista knew it would drop even further the closer they got to Edwina. At the same time, she felt a presence around her. Something out of sight, but close. Warm.

But of course, out in the marshes there was an uncanny sense of loneliness. It pressed in around them—an emotion that clung like fog. Nothing could be built in this part of the marshes, nothing that would stay, at least. Calista wondered how many buildings had sunk into the mud here. How many bodies were under her feet?

The thought was beyond terrifying, and Calista clicked on her flashlight, illuminating the path. She took out the map she'd brought with her, checking the directions. The scenery had changed since the map was drawn. Most of the landmarks had been claimed by the marshes since then, sunken below the surface. There were no trees or big boulders to use for navigation. But Calista could feel they were going the right way. She would just have to use her intuition to find Edwina's shack.

Calista looked sideways at Wyland. He gulped, clearly afraid.

"Ready?" she asked him. He nodded, his skin gray in the low light.

The two began down the path, their shoes squishing the mud along the way. Calista felt the dagger in her pocket, bumping against her side, but she didn't want to think about it. Not until she had to.

It didn't take long for the reeds to grow taller, the ground to get lower. It was darker with each step, and eventually, Wyland turned on his flashlight, too.

Soon, they would lose sight of the surrounding area. Calista looked back from where they had come, worried the path would somehow disappear. But she knew she had to keep moving. Especially when she felt a wisp of cold air. The hair on her arms stood on end and Calista quickly turned to find a ghost walking next to her. It was Devon Winters.

"You found me," he said, oblivious to the fact that he was dead. He walked slowly, dragging his feet behind him. Calista wondered if some part of him remembered that he was stuck.

She tried to smile at him, although his presence here in the marshes felt scarier than it did at her house. "Are we close?" Calista asked him, the glow of her flashlight shining through his body.

"I have no idea," Wyland said. "You have the map."

"I'm not talking to you," Calista replied, and heard him suck in a startled breath.

Wyland stopped suddenly, his eyes frightened. "Is it my brother?" he asked.

"No," Calista answered quickly. "It's . . . It's Devon Winters. He's here with us."

Wyland darted his gaze around before walking again. "Okay," he said tentatively. "Can you ask if he's seen my brother?"

Calista turned to the ghost. He seemed to be walking along with them aimlessly, not in any hurry. Not scared or worried. "Devon," she started, "are you with the other kids?"

"Oh, yes," he responded with a nod. "There are a lot of us here in the marshes. Hundreds." He smiled.

Calista was not comforted at the idea of so many dead people. It would only be a matter of time before they tried to contact her too. At the thought, she glanced out into the reeds and noticed some faces, pale with eyes reflecting in the dark like animals caught in the headlights. Dead, all around her. She quickly turned away.

After midnight, it wouldn't matter anymore. She wouldn't be able to see them.

"Are we close?" Calista asked Devon again, her nerves ratcheting up.

Devon seemed to think on it and then nodded. "Yes," he said. "The house is just ahead and to the right. You'll have to go underground to get in, though."

"Great," Calista muttered. "And I'm guessing none of you ghosts can help us?"

The eyes of the dead blinked at her all around the marshes, silent.

Wyland jumped, glancing around. "None of *what?*"

"Nothing," Calista told him. "Devon said the house is up ahead and to the right." Wyland breathed out his relief.

The shrubs got thicker, blocking their view of anything other than the path. Calista was worried she'd pass the old shack, but then Devon moved ahead of her, appearing to the right.

"Through here," he said, vanishing between the reeds.

Calista stopped walking, shining her light in that direction. It was a wall of plants, no path forward. The mud was thicker there.

"You're kidding," Wyland said, looking between her and the reeds.

"He said it's over there," she told him, her voice hesitant.

They waited an extra moment before they both walked over. Calista pushed aside some of the reeds to try to get a better view, but she couldn't see much. She'd have to take it on faith.

They were running out of time.

"Come on," she told Wyland, and stepped through.

The ground was soggy, clinging to her sneakers and giving her a fright. "Careful," she murmured back to Wyland as they picked their way through. Each step was more effort, the heel of her sneaker slipping off twice.

"Please don't sink," she murmured, her flashlight shaking in her hand.

Just up ahead, Devon would occasionally look back at her to make sure she was following. It only occurred to Calista for a moment that he could be purposely leading them to their deaths. She felt nothing but pure kindness radiating from his spirit. Hope. He wanted to be found, even if he couldn't articulate that.

And then, all the sounds of the marshes suddenly stopped around them—utter silence. Unnatural silence. The temperature plummeted. A deep ache began to pull at Calista's

bones, cramping in her muscles. She felt sick. She felt . . .
death. The house was close.

Calista swept her gaze around the area until she noticed
the slight rise in the mud to her right. Then, between two
thatches of bushes, she saw the top of a stone chimney,
crumbling with age and rot. The corner of the shack was
camouflaged with moss and plants, but she could soon make
out a dirt-covered glass window. She gasped with relief.

"There it is," she said, pointing. "Wyland!"

Wyland hopped through the mud to meet her. At one
point it sucked his sneaker right off his foot and he had to
double back, holding his socked foot above the mud as he
worked out his shoe and got it back on. He walked carefully
to stand next to Calista.

"Where?" he asked, his breath a white puff in the icy air.
He shivered from the sudden cold that had begun to wrap
around them.

Calista pointed just up ahead. When Wyland saw the top
of the building, his eyes widened.

"There's really a house under there," he murmured. "It's
really there."

"Can you feel it?" she asked him, her stomach nauseous.
"Can you feel that energy? It's . . . It's like poison."

"No," he said. "Well, I'm a bit angry, I guess. Uncomfortable."

"It's all around us," Calista said, her voice pitched low.
She reached into her pocket, her fingers grazing the moon

rocks and their zap of creation energy.

"Tranquillitas et stabilis," she murmured. *Calm and steady.* She repeated it, and then the sounds began to filter back in around her. The frogs, the soft whistling of wind. The pain subsided.

"Do you really think the kids are in there?" Wyland whispered, drawing her attention.

"We're about to find out," Calista replied, bolstering her courage.

She glanced once more at Devon's ghost, thanking him with a nod. He had begun to fade, slipping away from her sight. She didn't have much time left with her gift. She hurried then, moving toward the open window.

Calista made her way over to the side of the house, having to grip onto the roof that was half sticking out of the mud on her way to the window. The moss on the house was slick under her fingers, the wood breaking off when she held too tightly. But finally, she got to the window. It poked up from the mud, but only as high as her knees. She would have to go underground to be inside the house, just as Devon had told her.

It was dark, and Calista tried to shine her flashlight through the dirty glass, but the angle was all wrong. She had no idea what would be waiting for her inside. She took a deep breath, blowing it out in a steady white puff of air.

"I'll go first," Calista told Wyland. "But you should probably wait here."

"Not a chance," he replied. "But . . . you can still go first." Wyland scrunched his nose with embarrassment, but Calista had to laugh. She appreciated his honesty. And really, for a non-medium, he'd been pretty brave so far.

Calista squatted down and began to dig out the edges of the window just under the mud. Then she gripped it and tried to lift the stubborn pane. Wyland quickly came over and put his palms against the glass, doing his best to slide it up at the same time. The window was old—the wood squeaking and crackling as they moved it. Finally it gave way and pushed open.

Immediately, the smell of rot rushed out to meet them. Wyland groaned, waving his hand in front of his face as he backed away.

The energy slipped out next—slick, dark energy, like slime oozing toward Calista. Yes, Edwina had definitely been here. Her presence was soaked into the walls, the mud, the rooftop. This was her house. It was part of her.

And then a horrible realization hit Calista. What she didn't feel, and what scared her, was the other children. There was no scent of her sister's bubbles. Nothing to indicate that Molly or anyone else living was there. A blast of fear struck her.

What if they were like Thomas, scattered into ashes?

Calista's foot slipped through the mud and banged the edge of the open window, dislodging the glass at the top. The sheet of glass fell into the room, shattering on the floor.

Wyland grabbed Calista's arm to pull her back. She tried to catch her breath, still consumed by the dark thoughts.

"Are you okay?" Wyland asked worriedly. "Did you cut yourself?"

Calista shook her head no, afraid that fear would come through in her voice if she answered. She had to focus. After another breath, she stepped toward the window, holding on to Wyland's hand as she lowered herself inside.

The room was pure darkness except for her flashlight. When Calista's shoe touched the old floorboards, they whined under her weight. She stepped to the side, glass crunching under her heel, to make room for Wyland as he climbed down to join her.

The vileness in the air continued, but Calista didn't sense that Edwina was actually there. Which was a very good thing.

Wyland covered his nose with the sleeve of his jacket. "What *is* that smell?" he asked. "I think I might puke."

"It's evil," Calista responded, her heart beating quickly. Instinctively, she touched the handle of the dagger in her coat, but it brought little comfort. Aunt Freya would have been brave enough to use it, but even now . . . Calista worried if she could do the same.

Time was running out. Calista gathered her courage, and then lifted her flashlight to examine the small space. But once the room came into view, Calista gasped and reached behind her to grab Wyland's arm.

Because in the center of the room, spotlighted by her

flashlight, were Molly and Parker. The two small children were asleep and huddled together, the rest of the room submerged in darkness.

"Parker!" Wyland yelled. He started toward them, but Calista pulled him back.

"What are you doing?" he asked, spinning to face her. "They're right there."

Calista glanced around the room again, her light finding the symbols carved into the wood around the sleeping children. Three wavy lines with pointed shapes inside a circle. A similar pattern to the one she'd seen in the section on lost souls. And Calista had a horrifying realization.

"They're not really here, Wyland," she said, her voice tight. "Molly and Parker are between worlds right now— between the veil of the living and the dead."

"What?" Wyland breathed out, staring at the kids again.

Calista's heart sank with despair. At any moment, Edwina could pull them into death, or, worse, send them to limbo like her aunt Virginia. Then they would have no way to communicate. No way to pass on. They would be nothingness, forever.

Calista looked again at her baby sister, tiny as she slept. She wanted so much to gather Molly in her arms and bring her home to their mother, but she was scared to touch her. Afraid it might accidentally send her to the other side.

"Then what do we do?" Wyland asked, panicked. "How do we help them?"

Although Calista had planned on re-creating her aunt's spell from the summoning, she couldn't do it now. Not with her little sister right there, teetering on oblivion. She needed help. She needed her father before it was too late.

Calista closed her eyes. "Dad?" she called. "Dad, can you hear me?"

And just like she'd hoped he would, Mac appeared to her. She'd had a sense earlier, and was relieved to see it was true. Her father had followed her all the way from the house, watching over her. He was here with her now, no matter the consequences.

"Dad," Calista said, "I need your help."

25

MAC STOOD IN the small shack where his sister died all those years ago, his face pulled down with grief and fear. But Calista was relieved to see him. She also knew that it would probably be for the last time.

"Edwina has done something to Molly and the other boy," Calista told her father. "How can we wake them up? How can we get them here with us, on this side of the veil?"

Mac looked down at where the two kids were clinging together. "It's Edwina's spell holding them between worlds," he said clearly. "She's the thread. We need to sever the connection."

"How?" Calista asked again, growing impatient. There wasn't much time. She didn't know how close to midnight it was.

"We have to banish her," Mac said. "Banish her from the realm of the living. I know Freya thought she could destroy her, but Edwina is too strong. Even if you bound her, it would only take a flick of her wrist to send these kids to limbo. But a banishing spell, it might buy us some time."

The answer was not ideal, but Calista wasn't sure if she had another choice. Like a protection spell, a banishing spell was only temporary. It was a Band-Aid on a gaping wound—you would still bleed to death.

"What's your dad saying?" Wyland asked. "Does he know what to do?"

Calista turned to him, wanting to say yes. Almost wanting to lie to make it true. But she couldn't bring herself to do that. "Not really," she said somberly.

Wyland groaned out his pain. He started for his brother again, but Calista called his name.

"Wyland," she said. "Don't touch them. We should—"

There was a sudden shift in the air as a blast of biting cold invaded the room. Calista's flashlight slipped from her fingers, clanging onto the floor. The force of Edwina's presence blew the shattered glass along the floor, causing the light to bounce off the skidded pieces in a soft prism.

Wyland fell back a step. "What's going on?" he asked, his teeth beginning to chatter.

"It's her," Calista whispered. Her fear spiked, her heart beating wildly. "The Tall Lady is here."

Mac walked over to stand in front of Calista and Wyland, facing the center of the room. He lowered his head, fierce and ready. "Stay behind me," he told Calista. Even now, her father was trying to protect her.

A whisper of black smoke began to leak in through the slats of the walls, collecting near the circle where the kids were asleep. Soon, the smoke began to take a form, slowly edging itself out until it faded, leaving in its wake an evil spirit in a bright yellow dress.

Edwina flashed her sharp teeth at Mac in a devilish smile.

"As I'd hoped," she said. "You Wynns are a predictable lot."

"What do you want from us?" Calista yelled from behind her father. "Whatever it is, just let my sister and Parker go. You don't need them."

Edwina tilted her head to look at her standing behind Mac, tendrils of dark hair hanging over her shoulder. "But I do," she told Calista, mockingly. "Don't you see? They brought *you* here. To my land. To my home. You'll get to watch me kill *everyone*." She laughed, the sound piercing and cruel.

"Calista?" Wyland said from next to her. His voice shook in the cold. "What's happening?"

He couldn't see Edwina. Calista wasn't sure if that was more terrifying for him.

"Just stay quiet," she whispered to Wyland, looking over once. She could see he was frightened, but the truth was that there was nothing he could do to help, not at this point. In fact, she regretted bringing him at all and putting him in danger. "Don't draw her attention," she added quietly.

Wyland reached out to grip Calista's hand, squeezing it. Then he nodded and dropped her palm as he took a step back from the center of the room.

"Leave my children alone," Mac told Edwina. "Leave my family alone."

Edwina pretended to pout. "Sorry, Mac," she said. "You know, all those years ago, I would have taken you too. But you were so small. Not nearly as strong as your sister. But I want you to know"—she smiled—"I took Virginia Wynn's soul and I *devoured* it." She licked her red lips. "Delicious."

Rage radiated from Mac, flowing into Calista. The energy surged through her just like it had at the séance table. Her family didn't want her to use those dark emotions, but at this point, she wasn't sure she could resist. She hated Edwina. She hated her too much to stop.

"I'm not going to let you hurt them," Mac said, squaring his shoulders, ready to fight.

"You have no power here," Edwina said. "You grow weaker every day, clinging to some pathetic connection to your family. You are no threat to me, Mac. None of you are."

Edwina lifted her palms at her sides and the air in the room grew electric. For a moment, Calista gasped as it stole her breath. But then it eased, and Calista could feel the energy pulsing around her. Static shock.

"This can't be good," Wyland murmured from behind her, his hair standing on end.

The Tall Lady began a chant, her voice demonic and deep, and immediately Calista's father put up his hands in defense, groaning as if in pain.

Calista tried to understand Edwina's words, but they weren't in Latin. She had the sense they were Edwina's own form of conjuring—something evil that she created all by herself.

Mac took a labored step toward Edwina, but a sudden wind forced him back. It began to blow around the room, kicking up dust and making it spiral around them. The glass made small clicks as it spread along the floor.

Edwina stopped chanting and steadied her hateful gaze on Calista's father. Her features began to change, distort. Her eyes were all black, her skin pulled tight over her sharp cheekbones. She barely looked human.

"Come on!" she growled at Mac. "Let's you and I finish this."

And then, Calista's father charged ahead. He grunted out a noise of exertion as he rushed toward the Tall Lady, like a football player going in for a tackle. Calista watched in terrified anticipation, yelping out her concern when the two spirits crashed together.

Mac rammed his shoulder into Edwina's stomach, her body folding over his and rolling off his back. The entire house shook, and both Calista and Wyland lost their balance and fell to the floor. Dirt poured in from the slats on the wall. It occurred to Calista that the structure could cave in at any second.

Despite his size, Mac was no match for Edwina. The Tall Lady swung out her hand and knocked him back, sending

Mac into the wall with a thud. More clumps of earth fell to the floor. Out of the debris, worms twisted and small bugs skittered away from Calista. The walls wouldn't be able to hold back the marshes much longer if the battle continued. They would all be crushed.

Calista looked over at her sister again, so small and fragile. She'd promised to protect her. Molly needed her now more than ever. She had to do something.

"Stay down," Calista told Wyland.

Calista couldn't even imagine what he was thinking as he felt the spiritual feedback and swaying shack, his footing unsteady. And yet, he had no idea of the real battle going on around him.

"What are you going to do?" Wyland asked, assessing the chaos in the room.

"I'm going to save my family," Calista said between breaths as she climbed to her feet next to him.

And then suddenly, Edwina's hand shot out to grab Mac's spirit by the throat. His eyes widened, his expression frozen in fear. Edwina had the power to destroy him.

"Stop!" Calista screamed.

There was a shimmer in the air, a familiar smell of warm summer days, even though the room was freezing cold. And then Grandma Josie appeared.

Calista gasped at seeing her grandmother, her shawl around her shoulders, her small frame tense, with her hands in fists at her sides.

"Gran, what are you doing?" Calista asked, scared for her. But her grandmother held up a finger to silence her as she put all her focus on the Tall Lady.

"I hope she's our backup," Calista heard Wyland say from behind her.

"Let him go, Edwina," Grandma Josie called, her voice echoing off the walls of the small room. The sound was drenched in maternal power, strong enough to cut through any noise.

The dark spirit turned, startled to find Calista's grandmother in her shack. At first, Edwina seemed to falter, and Mac managed to get free.

He darted over to his mother. Grandma Josie stood her ground, her chin tilted upward. She motioned for Mac to get behind her. But before he could, Edwina took in a huge breath and opened her mouth impossibly wide to let out a bloodcurdling scream.

It was something otherworldly, the depths of hell. Even Wyland covered his ears on the floor, even though there was no way he could actually hear the sound. Just the vibration of it.

As Mac began to turn back toward Edwina, she shot forward, hand outstretched.

And before any of the Wynns could even react, the Tall Lady slashed her black nails across Mac's face, a single curse on her lips as she tore through his skin.

"Limbus . . ."

The world stopped. For Calista, everything stopped.

Mac stood a long moment, only the sound of Calista's shocked breathing in the air. Edwina grinned and moved back to stand over the children. Grandma Josie's fists unclenched, shaking, at her sides. No one spoke.

Slowly, Mac met his mother's eyes and then turned toward Calista. When he did, a whimper escaped from between her lips. The slashes Edwina had made in his skin were bleeding black ashes as her father slowly came undone.

"Dad?" Calista said in a small voice.

Mac blinked heavily and took a step toward her, his arms outstretched. Calista felt a surge of power, more than she'd ever had, at the sight of her injured father. She reached out too, and then, suddenly, they met, and their fingers touched. For the first time since he'd died, she *felt* him.

Calista's eyes widened and her father looked down at their hands. He smiled, his skin peeling away to float into the air. Quickly, he pulled Calista into a hug and she held him tightly, crying out as she did.

She could feel him. For so long, all she had wanted was to hug her father goodbye. And now she could actually feel him.

"Daddy," she whimpered. "Daddy, don't leave."

Mac sniffled, running his hand down the back of her hair. "You're amazing, Calista Wynn," he said, his voice echoing and growing further away. "I'm so proud of you. I'm so proud."

Calista pulled back so she could look at him, holding on to his arms. He was drifting away. Disintegrating. But even as he did, Mac held her and smiled.

"You can still stop her," Mac said. "There's still time. I know you—"

"I love you, Dad," Calista said, her words barely a whisper.

"Happy birthday, my girl. You're going to have an incredible life, I can feel it." He put his hand over his heart. "I really can." The char raced along his face, pulling away his mouth and sending it into ashes.

Quickly, Calista put her hand to his other cheek, hoping to hold him in place. Keep him. "Daddy, wait!" she cried. "Please!"

Mac Wynn exploded in a cloud of black ash, his soul scattering throughout the room.

26

CALISTA FELL BACK a step, and almost collapsed, but Wyland was already standing behind her to steady her. He was looking around the room at the scattering of black soot, clearly confused but understanding enough to know what had happened.

He didn't try to comfort Calista. He just kept her steady.

When Calista finally lifted her damp eyes to the room, she saw Grandma Josie standing there, her face drained of color, her shoulders slumped in defeat. She was speechless.

Then across the room, the Tall Lady laughed.

"Two of your children, old woman," Edwina said to Grandma Josie. "But that won't be the end of it." She bent down to run the back of her nails slowly along the cheek of a sleeping Parker. "You love this town so much. Even after how they've treated you," Edwina continued. "They dismissed you, Josie, and yet you've always protected them."

"They need protecting sometimes," Grandma Josie said, her voice cold. Steady.

Edwina looked up from the sleeping boy. "I'm going to take all the children," she said defiantly. "Make them pay for what their kin did to me. Nothing can stop me; nothing in this world is powerful enough to stop me." She looked at Calista. "That includes your auntie, little girl. Too many years out of practice, I suppose. I'll enjoy telling her that when I kill her next."

Calista felt half out of her mind. Edwina had beaten them. She had taken her aunt Virginia's soul, and then her father's. She'd take them all. For a brief moment, Calista even felt like giving up. She'd lost him. She'd lost her father.

But then her gaze touched on her little sister, still curled up on the floor. So innocent and with so much to live for.

"Molly," Calista whispered, the name giving her strength. It was all for Molly. She had to save her.

She thought quickly. Edwina had said, "Nothing in this world is powerful enough to stop me." Calista heard the words echo in her head again. *Nothing in this world. This* world.

There was an answer, a sense of a way out of all of this. Calista could smell birthday candles, just blown out.

"There's still time," Mac had told her.

There's still time! Calista thought suddenly.

Anxious, Calista quickly looked back at Wyland. "What time is it?" she demanded.

"What?" he seemed confused by the subject change, but distractedly checked anyway. "It's five minutes to midnight," he told her.

Calista gasped out her relief and swung around to face the Tall Lady. She knew what she had to do. And for a moment, she thought maybe she had always known it would end here among the smell of mud and soot.

"What if we make a trade?" Calista suggested loudly, drawing Edwina's attention.

Grandma Josie seemed startled by the offer and eyed Calista carefully, trying to understand. And then she tilted her head in approval.

"What could you possibly have to offer me, little girl?" Edwina asked with a laugh.

"My soul," Calista said, and gulped. "Take me in exchange for them." She motioned to the sleeping children at Edwina's feet. "I have more power than them combined."

The Tall Lady looked Calista over and then shook her head as if embarrassed for her. "I can see you weakening as we stand here," she said. "Do you have any idea who I am and what I can do? How insignificant you are in comparison?"

Edwina looked over at Wyland and smiled. Then she held out her hand and flipped her wrist. When she did, Parker Davis's small body rose from the floor like a marionette puppet, his arms hanging loose and outstretched, the boy's head lolling to the side.

Wyland cried out a horrified sound and grabbed Calista's shoulder. For her part, Calista knew she didn't have time to explain any of this to him. Couldn't explain what she had to do. She took a step forward, out of his grasp.

"I know you're powerful," Calista said, placating her. "The most powerful medium to ever exist. But that boy has no power at all. He can't do anything for you. Let him go. Take me instead, both Wynn girls, and show my grandmother how truly awful you are."

Grandma Josie stood by and said nothing, watching on in anticipation.

Edwina ran her tongue along her sharp teeth, intrigued at the idea of hurting Grandma Josie. She glanced at the dangling boy.

"You'd give yourself up for this stranger?" Edwina asked, turning to Calista again.

Calista nodded, taking another step toward the center of the room.

Edwina laughed, the sound piercing. "You are just like your grandmother," she spat at her. "Weak. And useless."

Calista let Edwina hurl her insults, but she wasn't sure how much longer she had until her birthday. Moments. Her powers were fading quickly. Even Calista's vision of the Tall Lady was starting to dissipate at the edges.

Then she felt a warm hand slip into hers. She looked sideways, finding her grandmother smiling at her, touching her. Grandma Josie pressed her lips into a soft, loving smile.

"Our time is almost up," Grandma Josie said quietly. "But I love you, dear girl." Calista sucked in a mournful breath, but Grandma Josie shook her head. "You'll be okay." She squeezed her hand. "Now you go on and forget everything your aunt Freya or I ever told you about holding back. You go on and save them. For all of us."

Tears dripped onto Calista's cheeks, a goodbye on her lips. But then she heard a thud as Edwina dropped Parker to the floor. The boy didn't even stir.

Grandma Josie's spirit faded, her hand disappeared from Calista's. Her ability to see her grandmother had gone, but left behind was a surge of warm energy still coursing through her body.

The Tall Lady sighed. "I'll take your trade," she announced. "But it won't save your sister."

Calista wiped quickly at the tears on her cheeks and turned toward the spirit. "Spare Parker," she said quickly, even as Edwina continued to fade from Calista's vision. "Do that, and I won't fight. I'm . . . I'm all yours."

With the swipe of her hand through the air, Edwina sent Parker's unconscious body sliding across the floor toward his brother. Wyland quickly gathered him up and moved back toward the wall with him, looking wildly around. Calista could feel Wyland's fear, but even that sense was fading.

With only a moment left, she walked right to Edwina and looked up at the evil spirit towering over her.

"I wish you had stayed buried in the swamp," Calista

said, tears spilling onto her cheeks.

She was scared. But she didn't try to push that feeling down, to hide her emotions in order to think more clearly. She didn't set aside her grief. She didn't even try to be strong like her aunt had taught her.

Instead, Calista let herself *feel*. She called to her heart absolutely all of it—her love for her sister and mother. Her love for her father and grandmother. The unspeakable grief from their deaths. The deep sadness of their loss. She let herself feel the anger that her life had worked out this way and the frustration that no one understood how much she was struggling.

Calista was bursting with emotion, but as the waves of pain left and receded, all that was left was love. A love so big, it crossed any reality.

Calista closed her eyes and channeled all of that energy.

The Tall Lady smiled with sharp teeth, a smile impossibly wide as she readied herself to devour Calista's soul. She raised her palm and began to draw it out of her body. As she did, Calista was hit with the most indescribable pain she'd ever felt. She cried out, overcome by a sensation like her skin was being separated from the muscle, her bones being pulled apart. The pain was so great, she shut down—felt herself being stripped away.

Calista hung limply, half off the ground as Edwina drained her life force, her soul. Her body vibrated as her power fed Edwina, the Tall Lady growing full with it. Blood seeped from Calista's nose, her fingers and toes gone numb.

Along with the draining, Calista could feel Edwina's curse beginning to take effect. The thirteen by thirteen curse, the thing Calista had always feared most. Edwina would devour it now, dooming herself by swallowing her own spell.

But was it already too late? Calista felt herself slipping away with the curse still inside her.

I love you, Dad, Calista thought again as she slid toward death. *And I love you, Gran.* But then Calista's thoughts turned toward her little sister, the idea of Molly growing up without her. The unimaginable grief her mother would feel at losing her. She had always thought she had to be strong for her family, but part of that meant being present. She couldn't leave them. She had to fight—as long as she could.

Calista didn't want to die. She wasn't going to die here. Not in this place.

On her last gasp, Calista surrounded herself in her family's love, a bright light in a darkened room. Power surged into her, like a lightbulb suddenly glowing too bright before it popped. And when it did, Calista screamed and sent that surge of power directly into Edwina, the Wynn curse slamming into her like a freight train as a beam of light burned a hole in the spirit's chest.

And just as the last of the light poured out of Calista, it happened. Midnight struck, and the curse enacted. Only now . . . it wasn't Calista's curse. It belonged to the Tall Lady.

Edwina choked on it, clutching her own throat. She

released Calista, who fell to the floor with a thud, her powers gone but her life still intact. She was alive.

Exhausted and barely conscious, Calista looked up at the evil spirit in the yellow dress. Edwina's eyes were wide as if she was still processing what had happened. Searching. Scared.

And then, her skin began to crack like a broken mirror.

"What have you done?" Edwina demanded, her voice pitched like nails on a chalkboard.

But she was no longer a spirit, she was on the living side of the veil. Edwina held up her palm toward Calista, but nothing happened. She had no power. More cracks raced over her skin.

Calista forced herself to sit up. She was weak, but she smiled anyway as she got to her feet.

Edwina had absorbed her own curse, draining herself of all her power. Without that power, and with her body long dead, her soul had nowhere to go. After generations of dealing in darkness, she was rotten from the inside out. She couldn't stay in this realm or any other. There was no love to hold her in place. Only revenge and hatred, which had no weight at all in the afterlife.

"You'll never hurt my family again," Calista said as Edwina continued to crack. "And you'll never harm the children of Meadowmere again. You are banned from this world, Edwina Swift." She reached into her coat pocket to take out her aunt Freya's dagger.

Calista stood, strong and brave.

Edwina opened her mouth to scream. But when she did, no sound came out. She was powerless.

Calista held up her aunt's knife and then threw it at Edwina. When it hit her, the Tall Lady shattered like glass and fell in pieces on the floor. There was a sizzle as those pieces began to evaporate. They became a cloud of black smoke, intertwined and dissipating before it was carried back out the small window to the swamp.

Edwina Swift was finally gone. Gone forever.

27

WITH EDWINA DEAD, Calista immediately rushed over to Molly, who was still curled up on the floor. She slipped off her jacket and wrapped it around the sleeping girl. As she touched her, Molly began to stir. Grateful, Calista gathered her in her arms to hug her. Molly whimpered a moment, but then hugged her sister back.

"It stinks in here," Molly said in a tiny voice. Calista laughed, wiping happy tears off her cheeks.

Calista heard movement and looked back to see Wyland with Parker, who had also woken up. The boy was filthy, his hair matted, and dirt and small cuts marked his cheek from when he had slid across the floor. But he looked up at his older brother, completely confused.

"Where's Mom?" he asked, on the verge of tears.

"She's on her way," Wyland said, hugging him. He looked over his shoulder at Calista and smiled. "I called the police," he told her. "I figured that now we could use their help."

Calista nodded and smiled back. "Good idea," she told him. She was grateful he was there for them. For her. Even if he didn't have any supernatural gifts.

Just as Calista turned back to Molly, she noticed the glow from her flashlight had shifted in the room, illuminating one of the dark corners. Calista gasped, setting her sister down as she got to her feet.

In the corner of the room were two boys, sitting on the floor and glancing around as if dazed. Calista laughed out her surprise, her relief. She recognized them.

Thomas Hassel was the first to notice her, although he didn't seem to remember they'd already met. "Hi," he said, and then touched his throat, clearing it once. He looked around. "Where are we?"

Calista couldn't help feeling a little weepy. Even if Thomas didn't remember her, she was so happy to see him. And he was *alive* this time. Next to Thomas, Devon looked equally shocked as he sat silently, glancing around the room.

Molly got to her feet, hugging Calista hard as she did.

"How are they here?" Calista murmured to herself as she looked at the boys. She had thought they were both gone forever.

"You brought them back from limbo," a voice said.

When Calista turned, she was stunned to see a girl spirit about her age standing there. It took a moment before she recognized her. She fell back a step, overcome.

"Aunt Virginia?" she asked. She paused. "Wait, how am I seeing you? My gifts——"

Virginia smiled widely, reminding Calista of the happy picture she'd seen of her aunt in the photo album. Virginia motioned toward Molly, who was still holding on to Calista, her gift strong and pulsing in the shack—showing Calista the vision. Molly was powerful indeed.

"It's only for a moment," Virginia said, "but I had to say thank you. Thank you for freeing us." Behind her, other spirits appeared, eight of them—walking straight out of the walls of the shack.

Although Calista was happy they were free from Edwina's prison in limbo, she also knew they had no bodies to go back to. These children were all dead. The forever kind of dead. Even so, they appeared to be at peace.

Just then, there was another shift in the air and Grandma Josie appeared in the room, heading straight for her daughter. Calista cried out in happiness at seeing her grandmother again, and watched with joy as Grandma Josie and Aunt Virginia embraced, finally, after all these years.

"I've been missing you, Mama," Aunt Virginia said, her cheek on Grandma Josie's shoulder.

"Missed you too, my girl," Grandma Josie said with a watery smile.

Calista took it all in, appreciating the moment instead of dreading when it would end. She got to see her grandmother again. She got to see her one last time.

As if knowing she was watching, Grandma Josie turned to Calista and Molly. "Don't make a fuss," she said with loving sternness, "I'm just passing through." Grandma Josie smiled, looking happier than Calista had ever seen her. "I'm going home with my daughter now."

Virginia took her mother's hand. Grandma Josie's eyes were damp as she smiled at her granddaughters.

"You two take care of each other," she said. "You make the Wynn name proud."

Calista didn't want to cry and ruin the moment, but she couldn't hold it back.

"Now, now," Grandma Josie said softly. "You did just right, Callie girl. All that love you've been holding in—the kind that's mixed with grief and hurt, you let it out and it set us free. You've been strong for a long time. Too long. We shouldn't have asked that of you." She pressed her lips into a sad smile. "But now you don't have to hold it in anymore," she continued. "You let that love, even when it's the sad kind, shine on through. That's your gift."

The words were like permission, both healing and hurting, but ultimately, right. Calista nodded at her grandmother, tears glistening in her eyes. Calista's heart was no longer as heavy. Even though her worst fears had come true, in a way, she was free too.

"Thank you," she murmured to her grandmother. Josie

closed her eyes for a long moment, nodding in return.

"Bye, Gran," Molly called out, waving excitedly.

Grandma Josie looked down at her, beaming with pride. "Goodbye, my little jellybean," she said, making her laugh.

As Calista watched, Grandma Josie, Aunt Virginia, and all the ghosts that Edwina had stolen from Meadowmere began to walk toward the wall, disappearing into their peaceful afterlife before they even reached the wooden slats.

The room immediately began to warm, filled with only the living. Calista looked around, hoping she would see her father one last time. Wishing for Mac. But the spirits were all gone.

There was a sharp snap, followed by a thud. Calista jumped and looked around. Wyland ran to her side as if readying for another fight. But then clumps of dirt began to pour in through the cracks in the walls. The ceiling shook. The room was crumbling around them.

"We've got to go!" Wyland yelled, tugging on Calista's arm before racing to the window.

He lifted his little brother out, and then Calista passed him Molly. The other boys staggered over, still disoriented. Calista guided them forward and Wyland helped boost them through the window.

As the dirt continued to pour in, Calista's flashlight was quickly buried. The room grew dark as the wood splintered, the earth raining down. Wyland climbed out the window and then reached his hand back in for Calista. She looked up at him, framed in moonlight, as he pulled her out into the open air of the marshes.

Calista's sneaker had barely cleared the window frame when the entire shack collapsed in on itself. Calista had to quickly pull herself away to keep from getting sucked down into dirt, the mud pouring in like cement. The shack sank lower and lower until it disappeared completely, buried under the unforgiving marsh.

"It's gone," Wyland said, gasping as he looked around wildly. "It's actually gone."

Calista got to her feet, still shaking. She stared at the pit of mud and moss, relief making her smile, making her cry. It was over.

"It's actually gone," Calista repeated, out of breath.

She turned to Molly again, hugging her sister tightly as the blare of approaching sirens sounded in the distance.

When the police arrived, they had questions. A lot of them. Luckily, everyone was so grateful to find the missing kids alive that they didn't care that Calista was from a family of mediums. She offered an explanation of finding an old map and thinking that maybe her little sister had gone there. None of the kids could remember how they'd gotten to the old shack, so no one contradicted her.

Thomas and Devon were severely dehydrated, and Thomas had a cut on his head along with a splatter of blood on his collar. But otherwise, they all just had a few cuts and bruises.

Edwina's home was completely buried, crushed flat from the weight. Calista wondered if the portal had closed when the spirits were set free. She'd hoped her grandmother got to see it fall.

As Calista and Molly waited for their mother on the back bumper of an ambulance, both of them with clean bills of health, Calista kept her sister close. Molly didn't have too much to say, although she definitely liked the attention of the passing officers and paramedics. She also kept giggling and waving to the tall reeds of the marshes. Calista looked and was actually grateful when she didn't find any ghosts looking back.

"Hey," Wyland said, coming to stop in front of Calista. The circling blue and red lights on the emergency vehicles flashed over his skin. His parents had arrived and were over by the police cars, fawning over Parker as he stood with a wool blanket wrapped over his shoulders. "How are you?" Wyland asked Calista.

"I . . ." Calista thought about it and laughed. "I'm not entirely sure," she said. "But I'm glad we found your brother, and my sister. Thank you for your help."

"I didn't really *do* anything," he said, a little embarrassed.

"You believed me," Calista said with a shrug. "And you called the cops. So, thank you."

He nodded, running his palm over his hair. They were quiet for a few moments before he looked at her again. "So . . . does this mean you don't see ghosts anymore?" he whispered so no one around them could hear.

"That's what it means," Calista said with a flash of sadness. "It'll be an adjustment."

"Do you still know . . . other things?" he asked, seeming curious.

Calista stared back at him a moment and then nodded, guessing what he was wondering about. "Maybe," she said. "But you don't have to worry. Moira likes you too. She's the one who's been texting you. You should go for it." She shrugged.

Wyland laughed, turning away and covering his mouth. But then he scrunched up his nose and looked back to her. "You know," he said. "I'm actually kind of glad that didn't work out. I . . . Well, let's just say I'm not interested in Moira anymore."

There was a small flutter in Calista's stomach, but before she could investigate that feeling, Wyland lifted his hand in a wave.

"See you at school on Monday," he said, smiling.

"See you Monday," Calista replied, still a little shocked by the exchange.

As Wyland ran back over the path to catch up with his parents and Parker, all of them embracing, Molly giggled softly.

"What's so funny?" Calista asked, poking her shoulder teasingly.

"Oh, *nothing* . . . ," Molly sang out, and laughed herself silly.

"Molly?" Nora called, her voice shaking as she stepped out from her car, parked on the other side of the ambulance. "Calista?"

"Mom!" both girls yelled, and rushed in her direction.

Nora was beside herself with relief. She dropped right to her knees in the mud and put her hands on both sides of Molly's cheeks, looking her over. She then did the same to Calista before hugging them both tightly.

"Oh, my girls," she said. "Thank you, Mac."

The mention of her father sent a shot of pain through Calista's heart. She realized then how often her mother would just speak to Mac, expecting him to be there, but never actually seeing him. She took his presence on faith. And now, Calista would have to do the same.

An officer called to Nora from one of the police cars. Their mother nervously looked back at her girls, as if afraid to take her eyes off them for even a second. Calista motioned for her to go ahead.

"We'll be fine for five minutes, Mom," she said, making her mother smile.

"Don't move," she ordered. "I'll be right back." She patted Calista on the hand before jogging toward the officer.

As her mother left, Calista looked around again, taking in the crowds of people, the flashing lights. But there was only one person she was looking for—one last glimpse she was hoping to get.

"Dad?" she whispered ever so quietly. "Dad?"

"He's not here, Callie," Molly said with a knowing nod. "Daddy's not here anymore."

28

THE NEXT FEW days were a blur for the Wynn family. Although they didn't do any interviews with the press, they had some meetings with investigators. In the end, the police thanked both Calista and Wyland for their bravery but warned them to leave the investigations to the police.

A few days later, the Wynns got the news that Aunt Freya would be coming home from the hospital. Nora had spent all day making another rhubarb pie and Grandma Josie's chicken soup recipe, to which she added tomato sauce.

On her first night home, Calista helped her aunt pull out her chair at the kitchen table, holding her good arm as she slowly lowered her aunt into her seat. Calista had already told her everything that happened at the old shack, including Grandma Josie leaving with Virginia.

"It was time for Mom to go," Freya had murmured with tears in her eyes. "Same with Mac. But they'll be waiting for us. I'll see them soon enough." After a moment, she added with a sly smile, "Now I told you that dagger would work, didn't I?"

Calista and her aunt also discussed Molly and whether she would keep her gifts after the age of thirteen now that the curse was over. It was possible, Aunt Freya supposed. But only time would tell.

After Calista poured her aunt a glass of iced tea, she helped her mother bring the food to the table.

Things had changed quite a bit since Calista lost her gifts. She could still sense things, emotions, auras, maybe even do a little fortune-telling, but the ghosts were definitely all gone. Instead, she'd hear Molly talking to them. Laughing or demanding they quiet down because she was trying to sleep. Her sister was already pretty deft at handling unruly spirits.

There were no longer extra places set at the kitchen table either. When her mother first stopped leaving a setting for Mac and Josie, Calista reminded her that she'd forgotten. But Nora just smiled.

"We need to be living. Here, now. The four of us," she'd said, brushing her daughter's hair back. "That's all the spirits want for us, to live our lives as long as we have them. No need to hold a place for them anymore."

Calista didn't like the idea at first. She didn't like any of it. But Grandma Josie had told her to feel it all. No more hiding from the emotion. No more being too brave.

She mourned her father now, understanding that she

hadn't done so in the past. And it *hurt*. Losing her father was the most painful thing Calista had to go through, even if it was happening two years later.

"It's good to feel the sadness," Freya said, nodding along. "It reminds you of what a gift it is to smile."

And Calista felt a lot, almost all at once. Sometimes it was even hard to breathe through the pain. On those nights, she'd crawl in bed with her mother and let her hold her while she cried.

"It's time you let it out," Nora would whisper. "It's time."

And although it all still hurt, Calista was starting to move on. Several neighbors and their kids had come by the house to check on the family, bringing them enchiladas and chicken dishes. A girl from Calista's class asked to hang out after school and they ended up spending hours in the neighborhood, riding bikes until the streetlights came on.

Wyland invited Calista to join his table in the cafeteria along with a few other friends. And it was nice that Calista didn't have to eat lunch alone anymore. Wyland had turned out to be a really great friend.

And yet, Calista still felt alone sometimes. It was a strange sensation, being surrounded by the living. It wasn't nearly as intrusive. She missed the closeness she'd had with the dead, but of course, those weren't the kind of words she'd ever say out loud.

"This soup is great, Nora," Freya said at the dinner table,

slurping another spoonful as she moved gingerly. "Better than Mac's ever was."

Nora laughed. "Thank you. And I'm sure he'd be steaming mad hearing that." She looked around the room with a smile, but it faded when she remembered he was gone.

That took some getting used to. For a bit, her mother would still ask Calista to tell Mac something before she caught herself. Eventually, she stopped doing that. Calista thought maybe that felt a little worse.

Calista still talked to her father sometimes, talked out loud late at night in her room, hoping he could hear her wherever he was. Sometimes she imagined he was right next to her, nodding along. She would give anything for another moment with him.

She confessed that to her mother once, and Nora looked at her with tears in her eyes and said she understood. And Calista knew at that moment that she truly did.

Calista tried to be grateful for the moments she'd had with her father, counting every one of them as precious. Even the sad ones.

Suddenly, Molly giggled hysterically at the table. Calista looked sideways at her sister, who was thriving since returning from her brush with death. She was doing better at school, better at getting herself up in the morning. She'd even dragged her dollhouse downstairs into the séance room, where she now spent more of her time.

"What's so funny?" Calista asked Molly, poking her

shoulder to make her laugh again.

"It's Daddy," Molly said, looking at a blank space across the room. "He's making silly faces." She laughed again, nearly rolling out of her seat.

Calista gasped and looked at her mother, who met her eyes in surprise. Calista then turned to her aunt, who had a spoonful of soup paused at her lips. She sighed.

"Guess he wasn't ready to go yet," Freya said, mostly to herself. "Stubborn thing." Although she smiled slightly before slurping her soup off the spoon.

Calista turned to Molly, hope blooming in her chest. "Dad's . . . Dad's *here?*" she asked her sister, unable to keep the emotion out of her voice. And she didn't try to. She did just as Grandma Josie had told her, she felt it all.

"Uh-huh," Molly said, laughing again.

Calista looked over at the empty space, stared at it so hard that her eyes went blurry. But she couldn't see her father. Oh, how she wished she could.

"Hi, Dad," she murmured. She blinked quickly at the tears stinging her eyes and smiled.

Molly tilted her head, listening. Then she nodded and turned to Calista. "Daddy says he's proud of you, Callie," Molly said. "He says you *did good, Callie girl.*" She deepened her voice to mimic him.

Calista laughed, wiping the tears off her cheeks as they fell. She thanked Molly for passing along the message. Molly went back to eating, happily swinging her legs under the table. The room fell quiet.

Mac was still here, guiding Molly into her gifts. Not quite ready to leave his girls. He was here, even if she couldn't see him. Calista was grateful, but it didn't alleviate the heaviness in her chest. It didn't stop her from missing him.

And then Calista's mother slid her hand over hers and gripped it tightly. Calista turned to Nora, finding understanding there. Her mother had carried this same weight for a long time. After years of thinking her mother didn't understand her, Calista realized she was the only person now who really could.

"I love you, Mom," Calista said, squeezing her mother's hand in return.

Nora smiled, a wide smile, and nodded her head. "I love you, too," she replied.

And then, with tears in her eyes, Calista went back to eating her dinner. She smiled at her family around the table and told them about a project she was working on in social studies class. Told them about her new friend inviting her to the movies next weekend. And Molly, being mischievous, told Nora and Freya that Wyland had a big crush on Callie. Calista denied it, but she didn't need to be psychic to know it was true.

The evening went on, perfectly normal for an abnormal family. And every so often, Calista would look at that empty space across the room, still trying to catch a glimpse. Grateful that her father would always be watching over her.

Acknowledgments

This book has been in my head for years, or really, in my heart. Writing it helped me find some peace, although I still miss my grandmother greatly. I still miss her every day.

So this book is for you, Gram. Every book I write is for you.

I want to thank my editor, Kristen Pettit, for helping me bring this ghost story to life—pun intended. You believed in it from concept to completion, and I will be forever grateful for your support.

Thanks to my agent, Lane Heymont, who always enthusiastically encourages me to write the scariest stories possible. Thank you to my friends Amanda Morgan, Trish Doller, Diana Rodriguez Wallach, and Hannah Johnson. And thanks to my husband, kids, and three poorly behaved dogs for listening to my story ideas and allowing me to spend my weekends writing books.

Mindi Johnson, thank you for crying with me as I told

you the idea for this story and demanding that I finish it. You were right—it is special, even in our moments of grief.

And of course, thank you to my readers for spending time with me in Meadowmere among all the ghosts.